Marked
by
Temptation

Books by Deanna Chase

The Jade Calhoun Novels
Haunted on Bourbon Street
Witches of Bourbon Street
Demons of Bourbon Street
Angels of Bourbon Street
Shadows of Bourbon Street
Incubus of Bourbon Street (Winter 2014)

The Coven Pointe Novels
Marked by Temptation (a novella)

The Crescent City Fae Novels
Influential Magic
Irresistible Magic
Intoxicating Magic (June 2014)

The Destiny Novels
Defining Destiny
Book Two in the Destiny Series (Fall 2014)

Marked
by
Temptation

A Coven Pointe Novella

Deanna Chase

Bayou Moon Publishing

Bayou Moon Publishing
dkchase12@gmail.com
www.deannachase.com

Printed in the United States of America

Acknowledgments

Thank you to Anne Victory for everything. And to my AAD girls: you all are rock stars!

Chapter 1

Matisse

"I think your sex-witch pheromones are broken." Ashley smirked and took a long sip of her hurricane.

Glancing over her shoulder at Mr. Tall, Dark, and Holy-Shit-He's-Hot, I frowned. Had I gone too long between one-night stands? As a sex witch, I could usually have the pick of a club without even trying. All I had to do was put the intention out there, and the next thing I knew, I'd have him eating out of the palm of my hand. This one, though? He hadn't even looked twice.

"Mati?" Ashley waved her hand in front of my face. "I don't think staring is helping."

I blinked and then met her pale green eyes. "Do you think he's a witch?" That would explain it. He could have cast a protection spell of some sort that would make him immune to my magic.

She shook her head. "I don't think so. There's no magical signature, but I wouldn't say he's mundane either."

I gave her a confused look. "What does that mean? Is he an angel or intuitive or something?"

Ashley was a witch of a different sort. She couldn't cast spells. Her talent was in reading those with supernatural abilities. Not only could she sense a witch, but she could tell what kind of witch a person was or if they were an angel or psychic, et cetera.

"I'm not sure. I've never encountered his energy before." Her brows pinched as she concentrated. "It's so odd. Not a witch or an angel. Definitely not a demon."

I let out a small sigh of relief. That was a very good thing. Demons were nasty business. If he was a demon, I'd be obligated to send him back to Hell, and that would seriously ruin my plans for the evening. "So an intuitive then?"

She shrugged. "Probably, though I don't know what kind. So be careful once you decide you're done waiting for him to come to you."

"You know me too well." I grinned and tilted my beer bottle up, taking a swig of my Abita Purple Haze.

"If you're lucky, he won't know what hit him."

I laughed. "He's the one who's gonna get lucky."

She rolled her eyes. "Right. Like you don't enjoy yourself at all."

"Well…" I shifted my skirt so the slit landed in the middle of my thigh. If I needed to have sex to build up my powers, I sure as hell was going to enjoy it. I mean, right? How else was I supposed to deal with that?

Still, trolling for one-night stands in a bar sometimes meant ending up with under performers. There was nothing more disappointing than unwrapping the hottest guy in the place, only to find out he was a dud. Especially when I had spells to cast.

"What's the latest mission?" Ashley asked. Her careful, nonchalant question was so calculated I couldn't help but hide a giggle. Poor thing. She was dying to be more useful to the Witches' Council, but she'd never be more than an administrator. Her powers just weren't there.

"Special project for my sister."

"Oh." Ashley stared at me with interest but didn't ask any more questions. My sister was the head of the Angel Council. Any work for her was strictly confidential, which was unfortunate, because I could really use someone to talk to about it.

"Yeah." I downed the last of my beer and slammed the bottle on the table. "Time to get down to business."

"He's doomed." She raised her glass in his direction and saluted him.

Gods, I hoped so. I needed a power fix, and this guy was outshining everyone in the club. Smoothing my long hair back, I gave Ashley a tiny wave and sauntered across the bar. My target wasn't even watching me, but that didn't matter. The attitude was more about getting myself ready for the battle.

Just as I was about to make my move, a tiny waif of a blonde slid next to him and wrapped her arm around his waist. She cocked her head, swinging her long ponytail over her shoulder as she gazed up at him. Well, that made things more interesting. Competition had never stopped me before. His lips turned up in a slow seductive smile as he ran his fingers down the back of her exposed neck.

"No date?" she asked him.

He shook his head. "I'm not looking for one either."

Her lower lip jutted out into a sexy little pout as she said something about him needing the gentle touch of a good woman.

Oh Lord, help me. How desperate can you get? I squeezed between two tall, muscle-bound jocks and cast them each a flirty smile before turning my attention to the bartender.

"Matisse. Ready for that shot? Tequila?" Sally Ann gave me a knowing smile. She'd seen my routine a dozen times before.

"Rum this time." I was in the mood to mix it up. Casting a glance at Mr. Tall, Dark, and Too-Hot-to-Handle, I said, "New Orleans, Cajun spice."

She glanced at my future one-night stand and grinned. "Spicy indeed."

I laughed. Hopefully.

Sally Ann poured two shots, set one in front of me and held the other one over her head. "Time for body shots!"

A cheer went up through the bar. I turned around, holding my shot in front of me, letting them all know I was the prize. It was a well-known bar game that was supposed to be thrust upon unsuspecting patrons—usually bachelorettes—where the dude of the bartender's choice gets a free shot only if he performs a body shot and wins the approval of the crowd.

They never said no. Too much pressure.

Sally Ann scanned the bar twice, never once making eye contact with the obvious target. On her third pass, she slowed and then stared right at him, holding the shot out. "Do you think you can handle it?"

There was that seductive, confident smile again. "I think I've got it covered."

Sally Ann grinned. "We have a volunteer, folks. Now step back. Give him some space."

The crowd parted, forming a half circle around him and me. I set my shot on the counter and leaned back, waiting for him to make his move.

He accepted the rum from Sally Ann and placed the shot glass next to mine while he took a long perusal of my bare thigh. Then he gazed at my cleavage before finally meeting my eyes. "Any preference?"

"Any place that's already accessible," I replied, lifting my foot and resting my stiletto on the lowest rung of a bar stool so that my skirt inched higher.

That sexy gaze shifted back to my thigh, then my cleavage again.

A shiver of desire ran through my core. Yes. When we finally got to it, this was going to be fun.

The crowd hooted and hollered, calling out their body part of choice. My neck seemed to be popular, but a growing segment was angling for my thigh.

He grinned and nodded to a stool. "Take a seat."

I did as I was told, and with the way my skirt was positioned, my entire leg was virtually bare once I was settled on the stool.

He held the shot glass up high, letting everyone in the bar see it. Then he leaned down, drizzling a good portion of spiced rum over my thigh. With a wolfish grin, he lowered his mouth and licked every last drop.

Searing heat rippled through me, and I had to fight to keep from moaning right there in the bar. Holy shit. I wanted that mouth everywhere. I clenched my fists to keep from burying my hands in his hair. If I touched him, I might explode on the spot.

More catcalls erupted through the bar.

He stood up and moved in close with one leg between mine. "Still good?"

I nodded, unable to speak. If I did, I was certain I'd demand he take me to the back room right then and there.

Dipping two fingers in his half-empty shot glass, he eyed my neck and then my lips.

There was no way I was letting him kiss me in front of this giant crowd. Nope. Those lips weren't coming anywhere near mine unless we were alone and getting horizontal. My libido was too far gone for that sort of thing. I turned my head, giving him full access to my neck.

He brought his hand up and ran two rum-soaked fingers from the base of my ear down to my collarbone. When he dipped his head and his hot tongue met my flesh, I couldn't stop the tremor of desire. And the way his other hand tightened on my hip, I knew he'd felt it. Damn. He had all the power in this little scenario.

This wasn't how it was supposed to happen. By the time he was done, I was going to be dripping with pure lust. I had to find a way to get the upper hand here.

He held up his not-quite-empty shot glass and asked the crowd, "What shall we do with this?"

They reached new heights of excitement. The roar was so loud not one coherent suggestion was audible.

I took the glass from his outstretched hand and dipped my own fingers in it, then pressed them to his lips. His tongue darted out, and it was a good thing I was sitting, because either my knees would've given out or I would've thrown myself at him. The promise of what was to come later was almost too much to take.

Whoa. I'd never been so attracted to anyone before. That was really saying something, considering my history. And for once, I didn't even care about the power boost I was bound to get from the electricity sparking between us. No, what I had going on for this nameless guy was one hundred percent physical. Magic be damned. I wanted to enjoy everything he had to offer. But I couldn't do that if I seemed like a needy fool.

I pulled my hand away from his mouth and held my own shot glass up in a salute. "A round of applause, please," I said to the crowd. "He sure knows how to put on a show, wouldn't you say?"

Sally Ann cheered the loudest and did a fist pump. "Do I know how to pick 'em or what?"

The blonde, who'd been hanging all over Shot Guy, scowled at her. "That was rude. How do you know I'm not his girlfriend?"

"Because, sister, I've seen half a dozen of your type hit on him in the last two weeks." Sally Ann moved in and lowered her voice. "And I was right here when he said he wasn't interested."

Shot Guy sent the blonde an annoyed look and then glanced back at me with obvious interest. Good. I definitely had his attention. I moved in so our lips were only inches apart.

His dark eyes clouded with desire as he stared at my mouth. All it would take was one tiny movement in his direction, and his lips would be on mine. I was sure of it. I sucked in a tiny whisper of a breath and said, "Enjoy your night."

With a satisfied smile, I pulled back and downed my rum in one gulp. Then I swept past him toward the table I'd been sharing with Ashley.

The crowd erupted with applause. Had he been anyone else, I would've been sure he was following me. But something told me he hadn't moved an inch. I caught Ashley's eye. She gave me a tiny shake of her head. Damn. He was still at the bar.

Time for phase two. Scanning the room, I narrowed in on Brandon, an ex-fling who'd become a good friend, and smiled. Perfect. He was talking with another guy I recognized from our psych class. Psych Guy's eyes went wide with admiration when I silently took a place beside Brandon and slipped my hand in his. "It's time to dance."

He glanced down at me, humor in his clear blue eyes. "You think so? What about Shot Guy? Isn't he on the menu tonight?"

I smirked. "Forget him. He's old news. Or are you saying you'd rather sit here with no chance of getting laid?"

Psych Guy swallowed. I knew he thought I'd be taking Brandon home tonight. But after a few minutes of me sending Brandon's pheromones out into the club, he'd have his pick of the ladies.

Brandon tightened his hand on mine. "Hell no."

I grinned. I knew I could count on him. And why not? He'd get to go home with anyone he wanted… well, other than me. We were friends only. I didn't date. One-night stands. That was it. Otherwise my magic was too much for the poor guys to handle. But to be fair, Brandon did handle it better than most. He was a witch, too. Non-practicing, though. He'd said he didn't want to join a coven while in college. I couldn't blame him. Who wanted to deal with that crap while trying to get an engineering degree? I wasn't so lucky. My family made demands on me that kept me tied to my own coven.

Once on the dance floor, I pressed myself to Brandon. "Thanks."

"Anytime, doll," he said in my ear and wrapped his arms around me. "But it would be a lot easier if you'd just let me take care of your power needs."

I snorted. "I bet that would be a real hardship for you."

"Not in the slightest." He glanced at the bar and then tilted his head to whisper in my ear. "But looks like tonight I'm gonna be out in the cold. Shot Guy can't keep his eyes off you."

Finally. I was starting to think I'd lost my touch. I glanced up at Brandon and smiled. He really would be the perfect boyfriend if I was looking for a nice, stable guy to lean on. Also he was exactly my type when it came to physical looks. He was on the basketball team—tall, fit, and a well-defined upper body.

But he was almost too nice. And I felt like shit when I siphoned his power. It left him physically depleted to the point he'd spend most of the next day sleeping it off like a hangover. It was different with regular guys. It would take them a little longer to recover, but they were at least functional. Brandon's power was just too seductive. And I liked him too much to use him like that. Being a sex witch wasn't all it was cracked up to be.

"Excuse me," my future one-night stand said.

I stopped swaying against Brandon. "Yes?"

"My friend here was wondering if she could cut in."

I glanced around Shot Guy to find the waifish blonde making doe eyes at Brandon. I felt Brandon's body shake with a suppressed chuckle, and it took all my willpower to not smack him as I stepped back. "Of course."

Brandon leaned in, gave me a quick kiss on the cheek, and whispered, "Good luck with this one."

Smiling, I nodded to his new dance partner. "You, too."

Brandon held out his hand to the blonde, and eyeing each other with mutual interest, the pair disappeared into the crowd. I tilted my head, studying the tall, dark-haired guy standing next to me. "That was kind of you."

He shrugged. "It was either that or figure out a way to let her down gently."

"Not your type?"

Meeting my eyes, his lips curled up into that sexy half grin all the hot guys had perfected in high school. "I was hoping for more of a challenge."

"I see." I raised an eyebrow in question. "Who's the lucky girl?"

He chuckled. "You already know the answer to that." Then he held his hand out, offering it to me.

This guy was trouble waiting to happen. And I couldn't wait. I slipped my hand into his, and a second later, he tugged me with enough force that I spun into his waiting arms. His hands clutched my hips, holding me against his hard, muscled body.

My breath caught. Was he the one spelling me and not the other way around? He smelled of clean soap and rum. I couldn't help leaning in closer.

The song shifted to a faster number, but my partner kept our pace slow and sensual, barely swaying together. Everything was starting to heat. I wasn't going to last if he kept this up. My magic was already skating across my skin, dying for his lips on me again.

It scared me a little. I hadn't had a one-night stand in over a month. And I'd been working spells with Chessandra almost daily, so I knew I was depleted. But this response was shocking. It was as if I were dying of thirst almost. I had to have something to tide me over until we got down to business.

I moved my hands from his shoulders and curled my fingers into his hair at the base of his neck. He stiffened for a slight moment and then ran one hand up my spine, sending tingles to all my nerve endings.

What the hell was going on with this guy? I made a conscious effort to rein in my sexual energy. He was affecting me entirely too much.

"What's your name?" he asked in a husky take-me-to-bed tone.

"Matisse," I said, pleased when my voice didn't falter. "And you would be?"

He inclined his head and his rich, bourbon-colored eyes met mine with lust lurking in their depths. "The guy who's going to make you come in about five minutes."

Chapter 2

Vaughn

The sexy siren froze at my words, and I held back the grin trying desperately to break free. There was no doubt in my mind that if I hauled her to the bathroom, I'd have her screaming my name within minutes. That is if I decided to give it to her. Everything about her was screaming sex, from her long dark locks to her never-ending legs. But those eyes. That's where her heat was originating. I'd noticed them the moment she'd walked in the club.

My gaze landed on the Ken doll she'd been dancing with. Hell no. The last thing I'd let her do was go home with him. I didn't see her with Mr. Nice. Not at all. Shari would take care of him. Not that I thought Matisse had any real interest in that other guy. He was just a casualty in the mating ritual we'd started the moment we'd each decided to let the other make the first move.

"What did you just say?" she asked.

I chuckled. "I think you heard me."

"Presumptuous bastard, aren't you?" But she said it with a smile in her voice.

This was going to be interesting. "Only when a gorgeous woman picks me for a round of body shots."

She shrugged, not even trying to deny the game had been rigged. "I'm used to getting what I want."

There it was again. That undeniable sexual tension radiating from her. It called to me, made me want to drag her off to the nearest hotel room and do unspeakable things until she was gasping in pleasure. My groin tightened. Son of a bitch. My control had all but left the building. "Want to get out of here?"

She raised one of those perfectly arched eyebrows. "Not the bathroom?"

I scanned her body, taking in her jewel-encrusted designer heels, her barely there skirt, and the silky, off-the-shoulder top. She screamed seduction and class. "I get the feeling you'd prefer something a little more upscale than a graffiti-covered stall."

Her clever fingers curled into my hair once more as she leaned in, her warm breath tickling my ear. "What did you have a mind?"

"I have a place in the Garden District if you're game."

She glanced at the dark-haired girl she'd entered the bar with. A silent form of communication passed between them, and I assumed that was girl code for *I'm leaving with this guy. If I don't turn up in the morning, this is who you're looking for.*

There wasn't anything to worry about. I already knew she was some sort of witch. My stepmom and brother were both witches. I could sense their magic. Only Matisse's power was stronger than either of theirs. If she wanted to, she could probably spell my ass to Hell and back. But she wouldn't. She wanted me. No question.

I'd never had trouble attracting the opposite sex. My stepmom speculated I had some sort of magical power that drew women to me. I didn't know about that, but most nights I went out, I had more than my share of females to choose from. Real hardship, right? Only it wasn't nearly as satisfying when I didn't have to put any effort into the chase.

But this girl? She'd made it obvious she was interested and then promptly let me know I wasn't the only game in town. And even though I knew she wanted me, knew I would have her before the night was over, she wasn't handing herself over willingly either. If she were, we'd have already been in that bathroom stall.

"Maybe we should grab a coffee first," she said, tapping a message into her phone. "You know… learn each other's names before I let you get your hands on my black lace."

Leave it to her to wear black under her white skirt. "It's not your lace I'm interested in," I lied. Nothing sounded sexier than seeing her creamy breasts spilling out of her bra.

"I bet." She clasped her hand lightly around my fingers and led the way to the front door. I followed all too willingly. When was the last time I'd left a club with a girl for coffee? That was somewhere around never.

Out on the sidewalk, I took the lead through the residential streets that surrounded the university. "My ride is this way."

Matisse hovered close to me, the cool December air causing gooseflesh to rise on her arms. I wrapped an arm around her and tucked her close to my body. Damn if she didn't fit perfectly, as if she was made to be plastered to my side. Her hair smelled of berries and cream, making my mouth water with anticipation. If she smelled this good, what the hell would she taste like? I'd find out soon enough.

"This is it." I stopped next to the 2000 Indian Chief I'd gotten in a trade for a restored vintage model.

"Nice. Love the custom paint." Matisse eyed the black-and-silver marbled paint job, wrapping her arms around herself to guard against the cold.

I pulled my leather jacket out of the saddlebag and handed it to her. "Here. This should help."

"Thanks." She shrugged into the too-large jacket and smiled gratefully. "But I don't think I can get on that thing with you."

"Why? Too scared?" I said, with a challenge in my tone.

She laughed. "Not on your life. I've been riding since I was ten."

I sent her a look of admiration, and a ripple of that sexual tension seized me. "Really? And what exactly do you ride?"

"A Harley Sportster. It's easier to manipulate than your Indian and more reliable than a vintage model."

Jesus, this girl was sexy. "Then why can't you get on my bike? Is it the skirt?"

Her dark smoldering eyes met mine as she gave me a haughty smile. "No. I don't take rides from strangers."

A ripple of laughter reverberated through my chest. I never had told her my name. I held out a hand. "It's Vaughn. Vaughn Paxton."

She slipped her smooth hand into mine. "It's nice to meet you, Vaughn."

"Likewise, Matisse…"

"Call me Mati." Her smile vanished as she bit her lower lip.

"Something wrong?" I asked, not letting go of her hand.

"Oh no." Her sexy smile was back. "Nothing at all. Now, how about that coffee?"

At this point, I'd take this girl just about anywhere she wanted to go. The thought made me shift with unease. I'd gone from wanting a quick interlude in the club's bathroom to taking her back to my place for a much longer night of passion to settling for just about anything she was willing to give. I shook my head, trying to dislodge the thoughts. Whatever was going on wasn't normal.

"You okay?" she asked with an air of innocence that I wasn't buying.

"Yeah. Just clearing my head." I climbed on my bike. "Ready?"

She eyed me and my prized Indian. Then she nodded once, hitched up her skirt, and swung her exposed leg over the seat before settling in behind me. The fact that her bare thighs were clasped around me made me instantly hard. If I didn't get her back to my apartment soon, I was going to lose it and take her right there on the bike.

I pulled my helmet on and handed her my extra. After both were secured, I fired the bike to life and roared away from the curb, reveling in the way her lean body was pressed to my back.

Usually I preferred to ride alone as most of the girls clung to me, rigid and scared, when I leaned into turns or zipped between traffic. But not this girl. She kept a light grip, leaned into the turns with me, and whooped after I zigzagged past a line of cars stopped behind a broken-down SUV.

By the time I pulled up to my place, she was laughing and her hot breath on my neck was causing my blood to boil with intense need. Jesus. What happened to my self-control?

I turned my upper body and craned my neck, catching her lips in a scalding kiss. Her hot tongue caressed mine in a slow, sensual exploration. The underlying need was there, but she was holding back, enjoying the moment for all it was worth. I stifled a groan and pulled away. "Inside," I ordered.

She raised both eyebrows in curious amusement, then slid slowly off the back seat. "I thought we were going for coffee."

"There's coffee inside."

"What exactly do you think is going to happen once you have me all to yourself?"

I grabbed her hand and tugged her up the six steps to my front porch. I lived on the ground floor of an old Victorian that had been turned into a four-plex. At least I did for right now. In my line of work, it didn't pay to hang around any place for too long. Being a bounty hunter means I'm often a target for revenge. Especially when I'm usually asked to track down those with paranormal abilities. I'd had to move five times in the last two years.

When we were standing in front of my door, I yanked her to me and buried my hands in her dark hair. Kissing her roughly, I forced my tongue between her lips and devoured her until she gasped.

I'd claim every inch of her before the night was over.

She tensed, her hands digging into my biceps. But as I backed her up against the door and pressed my body to hers, she molded to me, her arms wrapping around me and tightening as she moaned with pleasure.

Yes. I could stand right there for hours, making her mine without ever taking a piece of clothing off her. But then her breath grew short and she pulled away, whispering, "Take me inside."

"In a moment." With her lips swollen and her eyes glazed with lust, I grasped her hips and jerked her forward, letting her experience my hard length. "Tell me how this makes you feel."

She didn't hesitate. There was no careful consideration of thought. Just pure unfiltered passion. "Like I want to wrap my lips around you and taste every inch of you."

Jesus fucking Christ.

I crushed my lips to her once more and then yanked away to jam my key in the lock. Once I had it open, I pulled her to me once more. Staring her in the eye, I walked backward through the threshold, never easing my hold. "Are you sure you're ready for this?" My voice was low, husky with promise. Or was that a threat?

She laughed and ran a red fingernail along my jawline. "Are you?"

Kicking the door shut, I spun us both around and pressed her against the wall.

Her smile never faltered. That confidence was so damn sexy. So alluring. Almost as if she believed she'd orchestrated this scenario. Hell, maybe she had. She'd been the one to make the first move after all. Well, if she started it, I was damn sure going to finish it.

With steady hands, I pushed my jacket off her bare shoulders. She leaned back, letting it fall to the floor. Lust hit me hard as I took her lower lip in mine and sucked gently until her eyes fluttered closed on a moan. Then with a willpower I didn't know I possessed, I stepped back, leaving her breathless against the wall. My gaze started at her sparkling red toenails, traveled up her exposed thigh, and then over her long neck and those intense eyes.

"What are you waiting for?" she asked quietly.

"For you. I want you to strip."

Chapter 3

Matisse

Amusement skated through me. This guy was perfect. Exactly what I wanted in a sex partner. Forceful, take charge, an alpha that had the control none of my previous partners could maintain. Not when my sex-witch pheromones were in full force like they were right now. I was depleted enough that I couldn't rein them in. I needed this release more than he could know. And not just because I had a spell to work tomorrow.

I wanted him. Wanted him more than I could remember wanting anyone ever. It was as if he had his own magic affecting me in some way. I didn't think so. At least I couldn't feel it. But if he did, all the better. I couldn't wait to get him naked.

Taking a step away from the wall, I slipped my heels off and stood barefoot on his perfectly polished hardwood floors. And then in slow motion, I carefully lowered the zipper on the side of my skirt. Holding the fabric together, I met his eyes. His long dark lashes lowered as his gaze narrowed in on my hands, anxiously waiting for me to drop the sleek skirt.

If I was going to strip, he was going to have to work for it. "Look at me," I ordered.

His gaze didn't waver, but after a long moment he glanced up. Raising one eyebrow, he pierced me with that look of dominance he embodied so perfectly. "What's the point in stripping if you don't want me to watch?"

My lips curled into a small smile. "I wanted to see that steely control you've got going on. It's..." I swallowed. "Hotter than you can imagine."

"Babe." He focused on my hands once more. "I've got plenty of control. What I don't have is patience." His hand clenched at his side. "Now, let's see that black lace."

His voice was firm, but also full of quiet seduction. The will to continue the power struggle fled. My hands relaxed and my soft white skirt fell silently to the floor.

Vaughn's dark eyes flashed with molten fire. Then he held his hand out to me. I took it and stepped out of the circle my skirt formed at my feet.

"Gorgeous," he said, and slipped one finger under the edge of my panties, teasing the sensitive flesh on my hip.

I was certain he was going to yank them down right there in his entryway. The hungry expression on his face said he wanted to. Instead, he pressed the other hand to my hip and glided it slowly up my side, bringing my silk shirt with it.

"So soft," he murmured and leaned in, trailing kisses over my bare shoulder until he reached my neck. A shiver tore through me at his light, spine-tingling touch. My body was alive with fire. I wanted him everywhere all at once. Instead, his gentle fingers were driving me insane. But I didn't dare demand more. Oh no. This was a delicious torture that I'd never experienced before. I'd stand there and let him explore my skin all night if he wanted to.

His other hand abandoned my hip and glided up my stomach until he was cupping my breast.

I sucked in a breath, wanting his mouth on mine. But he bit down on my neck, sending a ripple of pleasure-filled pain right to my center. I swayed and arched into his mouth.

"Yes," he breathed and lightly pinched my nipple through the fabric of my bra with his thumb and index finger.

Oh, Goddess. For a sex witch, I was ridiculously inexperienced in foreplay. Especially foreplay by a man who knew what he was doing. He squeezed my nipple tighter. I gasped as I tugged on his tight black T-shirt and splayed my hands over his rippled stomach. His muscles quivered beneath my touch as he once again bit down on my neck, hard, while his glorious fingers teased my other nipple relentlessly.

Intense fire shot from his bite, heating my insides to almost unbearable levels, making me claw at his chest, digging my nails into his rock hard pecs.

He hissed. "Fuck, Matisse." Then he caught my mouth in his and thrust his tongue over mine as he pulled my top up, lifting my arms as he went. We broke apart just long enough for the shirt to be freed.

Once it was gone, I pressed up on my tiptoes and clasped my hands against his face, meeting his lips in a slow, drawn-out kiss that was full of possession. I wanted to brand him. Mark him with my magic. Make him mine in every way possible. I could do it. It was a power I possessed. But that would make him no better than a sex slave, doomed to be at my beck and call for eternity. The spell was not looked upon kindly by any of the modern covens. Still, the desire to do it was there. Strong and pulsing beneath my breastbone.

The thought scared me. What an awful thing to do to someone. It was bad enough my witch pheromones could attract just about anyone I wanted. But to bind someone to me? It was unthinkable.

I pulled back, standing before him in the black lace I'd promised.

"What's wrong?" His gaze never slipped from mine. I admired him for it. If he'd been almost naked in front of me, I doubted I'd have had the control to not ogle him in appreciation. "Too much, too fast?"

I shook my head and wanted to laugh. If he only knew. Usually I was straddling my partner by now, well on my way to climax. "No. I just…" I took a good look at his flushed face and the hard outline of his arousal through his tight jeans. "Just wanted to savor the moment for a second."

His lips twitched and he crooked one finger at me. "Come."

I grinned. "I'm sure I will, just as soon as you're ready to take me there."

He let out a low chuckle. "Get your ass over here."

One step. Two. A few more and I stood before him, my hands resting lightly on his waist. "This needs to go." I tugged at his T-shirt. "I want to see what's under here."

Without a word, he raised his arms over his head.

I willed myself to not tear the shirt off and inched it up, letting my fingers graze his ribs. When the fabric bunched at his neck, he reached down and tugged it off over his head. He stood there, waiting for me to make the next move. "Tell me what you want," I said.

The storm was back in his eyes, and I suddenly had an image of me on all fours as he slammed into me from behind. My mouth went dry as another part of me instantly became wet. I was going to climb right out of my skin if he didn't touch me soon.

"Take your bra off," he said.

My fingers trembled as I reached behind my back and undid the hooks. The fabric sprang forward as I hunched my shoulders, letting the bra slip to the floor.

"Cup your breasts, feel the weight of them in your hands." His lust-filled tone was more of a command than any order he could've given me. It was the first time I'd been in a position to be the submissive in any seduction. And damn if I wasn't enjoying it. I did as I was told and closed my eyes as I rubbed both thumbs over my taut nipples.

"That's it, Mati girl." His tone went soft, full of affection and praise. "Touch yourself for me."

My lips parted as I stared at his bare chest and longed to mark him with my tongue.

"Now, pull those panties down. Let me see all of you."

My eyes snapped to his.

"You heard me. Do it now. Let me see that soft mound."

I couldn't believe I was standing there taking orders from someone I just met. Getting ready to bare myself to him while he stood there in his jeans and boots. But then, it wasn't as if I was helpless. I was a sex witch. Still, exposing myself was just as personal to me as the next girl. But the way he was watching and the fact that I could see him straining against his jeans had me slipping my panties down my thighs and letting them drop to my feet.

He stayed still and silent as he took in my bare flesh, marking me with those eyes. His fingers twitched, and I knew he was on the verge of losing control. I longed for that moment. Needed to see this man, who had so much sexual power over me, succumb to my touch.

"Do you want me to touch myself again?" I asked, inching my fingers down over my flat stomach.

"No," he all but growled. "I'll do the touching." Then he kicked his boots off as one hand worked the fly of his jeans.

"Let me." I reached out and tugged his zipper down, deliberately running my knuckles over the outline of his shaft.

He sucked in a shallow breath and reached out, caressing my cheek gently. The juxtaposition of the demanding lover with the gentle one only made me want him more. Holy hell. How was I ever going to make it through this?

His boxer briefs came down with his jeans and finally we were both bared to each other. I couldn't help but stare. He was beautiful in every way. Tall and lean, with a well-defined chest and muscular legs. I wanted to touch him everywhere.

He held out a hand. "This way."

I put my hand in his and ran my other down his arm as he guided me through a sparsely furnished living room and into his bedroom.

He stopped at the foot of the bed, running his hand through my hair. And when he kissed me, he pressed against me, his erection bobbing against my stomach. Everything quivered. Had I ever experienced this level of excitement before? No, not until right before I climaxed and my power was rushing through me. Is this how it was for normal people? If so, no wonder there were sex addicts. Much better than drugs or food. In that moment, I thought I could sustain myself just off his touch.

With one last nip of my lip, he pulled away and pointed to the bed. "Lie down."

The roughness in his voice only served to ratchet up my excitement. I did as I was told and waited for his next command.

He stood over me, raking that gaze down my body. He was beautiful. And I knew I'd do just about anything he asked as long as there was a promise of release by his touch. "Spread your legs for me."

Heat crawled over my face. Bashfulness was a first for me. Even though I was only in my early twenties, I'd had more than my share of partners. It was a given with my heritage. In order to grow my power, I had to feed off of sex. But I'd never let anyone be in charge before, and I sure as hell hadn't ever let anyone speak to me like that. If anything, it was the other way around. I usually called the shots. But that night, I willingly spread my legs for this stranger.

And when he climbed on the bed, positioning himself so his head was level with my sex, it was all I could do to not demand he put his mouth on me. But no demand was necessary. Just when I thought I was going to go crazy with wild need, he dipped his head and his tongue darted out, tasting me with such delicious, slow intensity my muscles clenched and power built deep in my core, sparking through me like a lightning rod.

Every nerve was alive and sensitive as his tongue worked his magic. I clutched at the soft covers, holding in the scream struggling to break free. Not yet. I couldn't come right then. I needed the magic to intensify, to build, to fill all my reserves. But when his fingers slipped along my inner thigh and teased at my opening, all rational thought left my head. Power be damned. All I wanted was him.

Chapter 4

Vaughn

I'd never been this hard in my life. With each moan and whimper I coaxed from Matisse, the more I wanted to be inside her, owning her, claiming her as mine. But I held back, denying the temptation. I couldn't let this woman have that much control over me.

Hell-bent on bringing her pleasure, I redoubled my efforts, and although she clearly was enjoying it, she appeared to be holding back. With each new stroke of my fingers and tongue that made her quiver in ecstasy, she shifted slightly to ease the friction. Why? She was a live wire more than ready to go off. And damned if I wasn't going to make it happen. Now.

Placing both hands firmly on her hips, I held her still, devouring her until her cries filled my ears and her body pulsed and trembled beneath my mouth. I glanced up, catching the utter rapture claiming her features. A faint glow materialized around her and the air shifted. It took me a moment to realize it was her power.

Sex witch.

Jesus. I was an idiot. No wonder she was so fucking alluring. It would also explain her confidence. But not her willingness to let me take control. Sex witches thrived on power. And control was a form of power. The fact that she'd yielded to me was mind-blowing. And fucking hot. It made me want her all the more.

"Vaughn?" she whispered.

I kissed my way up her hip and over her creamy stomach, stopping to concentrate on her right breast. Flicking my tongue over her nipple, I gazed up into her heavy-lidded eyes.

"That was..." Her back arched, pressing her breast deeper into my mouth as she moaned her approval. I didn't need her to tell me what the experience was like. I'd been right there with her, felt her struggle to maintain control, and felt her release when she'd finally been forced over the edge. And now she was pliant and more than willing to take everything I had to give. It was mind-blowing.

"Vaughn," she said again, more forcefully this time.

I smiled a wolfish grin and lifted my head, bringing my lips inches from hers. "Yes, Matisse?"

Her dark eyes flashed with mild irritation. Then she buried her hand in my hair and forced my head down as she kissed me with all the passion she'd tried to hold back earlier. I gave myself over to her, knowing she needed to call the shots in order to claim her power. I could do that for her. Was more than happy to.

She broke the kiss off but didn't release me. For a long, tension-filled moment, we stared at each other. Finally she licked her lips. "No more orders?"

I shook my head. "It's your turn to do as you will."

Those expressive eyes narrowed slightly. Then she placed both hands on my shoulders, and with sudden force, she pushed me over onto my back and rolled with me, pressing her breasts into my chest. She reached between us and ran her hand along my shaft. "I want you inside me."

My groin tightened as I gripped her thigh. "I'm ready for you, baby."

Her fingers closed around me. "So it seems."

I forced myself to let go of her hip and reached to the nightstand for a condom. "Here."

Her eyes gleamed with anticipation as she protected both of us. And then she was sinking her heat onto me, her lithe body shuddering with the pleasure it brought. When I was buried all the way in, she paused as she tilted her head back, reveling in the sensation. Every inch of her was smooth and perfect: her full breasts, her slim hips, her silky skin. I could've spent the entire night just exploring the wonders of her body.

But then she started to move. The delicious friction made me want to flip her onto her back and grind into her with rough force. I denied myself though. The torture of letting her set the pace only drove my need higher. I rested my hands on her hips and teased my thumb down as I watched myself sliding in and out of her.

So damned sexy. I couldn't stop the quick thrust of my hips, meeting her slow, excruciating pace.

"Oh, Goddess," she moaned and moved faster. Then that glow started again. Just a soft outline over her skin.

"Holy shit, Matisse." I couldn't wait any longer. The power that was building inside her, I felt it too. It was a hurricane of sensation that set my nerve endings on fire. I dug my fingers into her hip trying desperately to hold her to me as I finally slicked my thumb over her clit.

She gasped and stared at me wide-eyed. The glow around her intensified, and I was completely lost. I jerked my hips up, slamming into her over and over again. Her cries grew louder and wilder with each thrust. And just when I thought I couldn't last another moment, her muscles clenched and pulsed around me as her body went rigid. She moaned and ground against me one last time, holding me to her. Ripple after ripple of orgasm slammed through her until the light around her turned a brilliant white.

My entire body shook with tension as I let her ride it out. And just as she started to relax, I thrust up again, pulling a cry from her slightly parted lips. "Again," she whispered on a moan.

Another thrust. She let out a second moan, her head thrown back as she moved her hips in tiny circles. It was too fucking much. In one swift movement, I had her on her back, her legs wrapped tightly around my hips. I quickened the pace, slamming into her, making her cry out with each hard thrust. And then it happened. Her magic pulsed over my skin and seized me, touching me deep inside. Her entire body wrapped around mine, and I buried myself deep inside her one last time as a firebolt seared through me. I shuddered against her, losing myself completely in the release.

It took a while to come back to myself. I was lying on my back with Matisse's head resting on my chest. Her fingers were tracing a small circle over my abs. "Hey," I said softly.

She tilted her head up and smiled. "Hey, yourself."

I wanted to tell her how incredible she was. The words were right there on the tip of my tongue, but before I could say anything she rolled off, pulling one of the blankets with her. I watched her as she slipped into the bathroom. The sound of water rushing through the old pipes filled the room as I waited for her to return. I glanced at the clock. Two twenty-three a.m. Considering that I'd spent the day tracking the whereabouts of a sleezeball human who'd been selling spelled cookies to unsuspecting co-eds in an effort to get laid, and then climbed into bed with Matisse, I should've been exhausted. But I wasn't. I was wide awake and all too happy to contemplate round two.

The door swung open. Matisse reappeared, her face freshly washed and her hair brushed back. Her relaxed posture and small, satisfied smile pleased me. I'd do whatever it took to put that look on her face again. She bypassed the bed and moved toward the front of my house.

I narrowed my eyes. "Going somewhere?"

She raised her eyebrows in mild surprise. "Home?"

"What's the hurry?" I sat up, letting the sheet fall to my lap, ready to drag her back to the bed if I had to.

Her smile was back as she walked toward me. Reaching out, she pressed her hand to the side of my face and then trailed her fingers down the side of my neck. The gesture was gentle, almost romantic, and sent another ripple of lust through me.

She could touch me anywhere she wanted and I'd be ready to take her in seconds. "I've got class in the morning."

Dammit. College girl. And she sure as hell wasn't the type to do the walk of shame. I slipped off the bed and pulled on a pair of pants I'd discarded the day before. "Gotcha."

I followed her into the entry hall where all her clothes were scattered. I expected her to be a bit shy putting her clothes on after the fact, but she wasn't. The blanket fell to the floor, leaving her entirely exposed. I couldn't take my eyes off her. She was mesmerizing with her quiet self-confidence, so different from the hard-edged seductress she'd been at the bar. Even more alluring than before.

"If you keep watching me like that, I doubt I'll make it home tonight," she said as she clasped her bra back in place.

"Is that a challenge? Or a request?" I moved in, nudging her chin up with my knuckle, and before she could answer, I claimed her mouth once again. The kiss was slow and full of promise. The passion sparking between us hadn't diminished one tiny bit. Blood rushed to my groin, making me hard once again.

She chuckled and gently pushed me away. "I really have to go."

I let my gaze rake down her body, pausing to appreciate her ample cleavage. "You're sure?"

"I'm sure." Her answer was so final as she zipped her skirt up there was no use trying to convince her otherwise. I pulled my T-shirt on and was stuffing my feet in my boots when she ran a light hand down my arm. "Thank you for the nice night, but there's no need to take me back to the club. My friend is here to pick me up."

I glanced out the window to see a small white car idling at the curb. What the hell? She hadn't had a phone on her when she'd gone into the bathroom. "How did she know where to find you?"

"I used your phone. It was on the bathroom counter." She leaned in and kissed my cheek. "Have a good night."

She pulled the door open, but before she could stride out, I caught her wrist. "You're leaving? Just like that?"

She frowned. "What do you mean, just like that?"

This wasn't a place I'd been in before. I wanted this girl's number. Wanted to see her again. Hell, what I really wanted to do was take her to bed again as soon as possible. But I liked that she challenged me, too. It was a thrilling combination. "I've only got your first name. How am I going to get in touch with you?"

Her lips turned up in that confident smile again. "You'll find a way."

This time when she walked away, I let her. She was right though. I damned well would find her again. And sooner rather than later.

Chapter 5

Matisse

Ashley sped away from the curb without saying a word. I knew she was waiting for me to give her a rundown of my night like I always did, but I couldn't seem to find the words. Not this time. Vaughn had been something different. More. And yet, even though my power had reached new heights when I'd been straddling him, once we'd finished, my magic seemed almost fragile. Like it would slip away at any moment. On any other night, I'd be brimming with fresh energy, ready to cast any spell Chessandra wanted me to. Had I been that depleted? Something was off there, and I wasn't sure what it was.

But sexually? Whoa. There was nothing wrong there. None of my past conquests could compete. Not even close. Like not even in the same state, let alone the same zip code. I couldn't believe I didn't give him my number. Maybe it was self-preservation. Because I could've easily stayed there in his bed for the next week, except I really did have class in the morning and an appointment with Chessandra to work on her special spell. The last thing I needed was a distraction. Especially one I knew I'd drop everything for. 'Cause, whew. If he knew how much I still wanted him…

I shook my head. No sense in thinking about that now. I'd made the decision to leave it at an incredible one-night stand. If we managed to run into each other again, that would be one thing, but I didn't do relationships. Not when I used people for sex. It was wrong. Necessary for me, but wrong nonetheless. It seemed okay and bearable only when the person I was with was using me, too.

"Well?" Ashley prompted when it became clear I wasn't talking. "How was it?"

"Good." I stared out the window.

"Good?" She scoffed. "It's getting close to three a.m. What the hell did you two do all night? Bake cookies?"

I couldn't help the snort of laughter. "Definitely not."

"So it was better than good then?"

She wasn't going to let this go. I had to give her something. "If I were a dating person, I definitely would've given him my number."

The car swerved slightly to the right, but Ashley quickly recovered and straightened the car. "Did you just say what I think you did?"

I gave her a rueful smile. "Yes. Definitely second date... er, second hookup material."

"Remind me to write this down." She took a left onto the on-ramp of the Crescent City Connection Bridge. "I do believe history has been made."

I smiled even though I had a sinking feeling in the pit of my stomach. It had taken a great deal of will to leave Vaughn so soon after our joining. And then to walk out when he'd all but asked for my number... It was hard. But what was I to do? None of the females in my family maintained steady healthy relationships with the opposite sex. My mom couldn't even give me the name of my father. She hadn't asked nor had she ever seen him again. It was the life of a sex witch. It sucked.

When Ashley finally pulled up to our place in Coven Pointe, I placed a hand on her arm, keeping her in the car for a moment. "Thanks for picking me up."

"It's no problem. I was just hanging out with Brandon's friend. Nothing exciting to report." She frowned. "But I don't get why you didn't just shadow walk."

"I was conserving my energy." In addition to being a sex witch, I also worked for the Angel Council as a shadow walker. If I concentrated, I could slip into the shadow world at a certain point and slip out at another using only my mind.

Being a shadow walker also meant I could cross between our world and the one where spirits walked. It was the same world demons had to pass through to get in and out of Hell. Since my sister was the head angel in charge, fighting demons was her main concern. Having someone she could count on who could slip through the worlds was very important to her. I wasn't that crazy about working with her. Dealing with the shadow world and possibly demons wasn't exactly on my to-do list. But it meant my mom left me alone and wasn't asking me to do much with the Coven these days.

And since I was in college, that was a good thing.

"Conserve?" Ashley gave me her you've-lost-your-mind look. "Aren't you brimming with power right now?"

I shrugged. "It's a big day tomorrow." I was working with Chessandra, and that meant I'd need my strength. If I had any. I was feeling pretty light-headed at the moment.

Ashley frowned and then yawned. "Well, whatever. Can we go in now?"

"Sure." I slipped out of her Honda and followed her into the entry of our Victorian four-plex. We both lived on the top floor. Me on the left and her on the right.

"Need a ride to school tomorrow?" she asked.

"No thanks. My bike is back from the shop." I gestured to the gated driveway. "Brandon took me to get it earlier today."

She rubbed her tired eyes and nodded. "Okay. See you tomorrow night then." She disappeared into her apartment while I was still fishing my key out of my pocket. Only it wasn't there. Shit! It was probably on Vaughn's tiled entryway somewhere. Well, there was nothing else to do but break in.

I placed my hand flat over the deadbolt and called my power. It was there, brewing beneath the surface, but it flickered with instability. Damn. After my night, I shouldn't even have had to think about the spell. What was wrong? I *had* been working very hard with Chessandra. Maybe I should've given Vaughn my number. I was going to need another fix in no time. At least I had an excuse to go back to his house thanks to that missing key.

After a few moments, my power warmed my hand and I visualized the lock turning. I heard the soft click and strode into my apartment, exhausted. If I fell asleep right then, I'd be lucky to get four hours before my alarm went off. Mornings weren't my thing, so I took a quick shower and fifteen minutes later crawled into bed.

———

I'd missed class. Damned snooze button. It was early afternoon, and I stood on the bank of the river on the Coven Pointe side, waiting for Chessandra to show up. It was cold and the wind blew off the Mississippi as I gazed at the French Quarter, resenting my sister more than she would ever know. Where the heck was she?

The whole point of working for Chessa was so that I would have more time to devote to my studies. But so far I'd had less time, or at the very least, less energy. Chessa was obsessed with this new spell we'd been working on. If we didn't get it today, I was going to have to take a break from her. I had too much work to do.

I was a double major in business and fine art. I planned to run a store devoted to my two loves: witchcraft and art. I'm not much of an artist myself, but I'm fascinated with all the creativity New Orleans breeds. I had visions of selling any creation that paid tribute to witchcraft and witches of all kinds.

My mom hated the idea. She'd prefer I not go to college at all and work in her spell shop. No thanks. I'm not too excited about whipping up love potions and luck charms and then having to replenish my magic with random one-night stands on a regular basis. Not that there was anything wrong with that, it just wasn't my thing.

I pulled my jacket around me and swore. "Damn, Chessa. I can't wait all day." I had a test later for my accounting class. If I missed it, I'd end up on academic probation. And then Mom would most likely refuse to pay my tuition for next semester.

"Get over yourself. I'm right here." Chessa materialized out of the gray mist and walked over to me, smiling as if I should find her amusing.

I scowled. "You're late. Again."

One of her perfectly groomed eyebrows rose as her chestnut hair blew in the breeze. "Cranky? I thought you were going out last night."

My scowl deepened. "Ugh. You're so rude." Usually I was relaxed and easygoing after recharging my batteries, so to speak.

"Did it not go well?" There was real concern in her tone.

I waved a hand, dismissing her question. "It went fine. But I have a test later. Can we get to work?" I knew I sounded irritated, but I couldn't help it. All I really wanted was to live the life of a regular college girl. But that would mean forsaking my coven and my family. I wasn't prepared to do that.

"Mati?" Chessa asked. "You seem out of sorts. Want to talk about it?"

I blew out a breath, hating that I was taking out my frustration on her. She was the head of the freaking Angel Council, for Goddess's sake. The fact that she was taking time out to work with me one-on-one instead of sending a minion was a true testament to how much she cared about me and what we were trying to do. I pushed my frustration aside and softened my voice. "Maybe later. Sorry. I don't mean to be such a bitch."

She nodded. "Obligations suck. I get it."

A low chuckle bubbled up, catching me by surprise. Chessa would know. She was fifteen years older than me, making her only thirty-six. At the age of eighteen she'd been pressed into

service as a low-level angel here in our world. Angels didn't
have a choice. They were born into witch families and were so
rare that they worked for the Council or were shunned by the
magical community. She'd handled that well enough, but then
two years ago, she'd battled a demon and somehow in the fight
ended up absorbing the demon's powers. The experience had
made her the most powerful angel in the angel realm. Now she
was forced to be the high angel whether she wanted to or not.
Yes, she knew all about obligations.

"I assume that means you're ready to get started?" She
grinned, knowing that was the last thing I wanted to do.

"Yes. The sooner we do our thing, the sooner I can stare at
Professor Fallon's bald spot."

She reached out and took my hand. A second later, we were
standing in the shadow world next to the entrance to Hell.

Now it was time to really see what kind of power I'd gained
from Vaughn. I'd been feeling a little off all day, so I didn't have
high hopes. But there was no reason not to try. Except for that
pesky problem of potentially attracting a demon. Chessa would
kick its ass though. I swallowed my fear and concentrated on
the spell Chessa had taught me.

Magic stirred from deep in my gut. It was strong and almost
foreign, but powerful. More powerful than I'd thought it would
be. Relief flooded through me. My night with Vaughn had
replenished my magic even if it did feel a little weird. It didn't
matter. The power was there, and that was what I needed.

Chessa stood beside me, vibrating with her own intense
power. If she weren't an angel, she'd have had this spell com-
pleted weeks ago. Unfortunately, angels were too closely connected to demons to be able to modify any of their spells.
Demons were, after all, fallen angels. Of course if she weren't
an angel, she never would've learned the spell in the first place.
And it wasn't one she could teach to just anyone. It could be
used to open portals as well, if the witch was powerful enough.
It was far too dangerous.

I raised my arms and focused on the shimmering outline of the portal. Spells were mostly about intention. But some required special sayings or chants. This was one of them. "*Obfirmave.*" The light flickered.

"More power," Chessa demanded.

I closed my eyes and focused, imagining my magic sealing the portal shut.

"It's working," Chessa said softly. Then she started to chant a string of words in Latin. I joined in, having no idea what she was saying. It seemed she'd developed an ear for it after her run-in with the demon.

The more the light faded, the faster her words came. I struggled to keep up and to control my magic at the same time. It kept slipping from my psychic hold. Before long, I was sweating with the effort. My hold on the magic slipped. The light brightened and the demon magic rushed back at me, fighting with the power I was forcing into the portal. Pain rippled through me from the tug-of-war in my gut that threatened to rip me apart. Desperately, I reeled my magic in, unwilling to let the spell destroy me.

Then something snapped.

"No!" I cried as an invisible force slammed into me. My concentration fled, and I fell to my knees, clutching my stomach.

"Mati!" Chessa cried and kneeled beside me. "What happened?"

"It ah…" I sucked in a breath and forced out, "I think it fought back."

Her head snapped up as the portal flashed brilliant white and a shadow formed behind the barrier. "Son of a demon's whore," she cried as she jumped to her feet and glanced at me. "Stay back."

I scrambled to my knees and crawled away from the portal. There was only one thing behind that door. A demon. And it was coming for me.

Chapter 6

Vaughn

After Matisse left, I lay in my bed, breathing in the faint scent of her perfume, unable to find sleep. I could still feel the imprint of her body next to mine, and the sensation left me restless. The loss was wholly unfamiliar and very unwelcome.

When the clock ticked over to six a.m., I finally gave up and rolled out of bed. Thirty minutes later, I was showered, dressed in fresh jeans and a Henley shirt, and on my way to the garage. No one else would be there, but that was part of the appeal. Tinkering with the bikes would push the sexy witch from my mind. Damn. I hoped so anyway, because otherwise I'd be compelled to put a trace on her, and if that wasn't crossing the line into creepy stalker, I didn't know what was.

I parked my Indian in the shop's lot and walked the four blocks to the neighborhood coffee shop. The moment I stepped through the door, I swallowed a groan. That chick, what's her name? Norma? Norah? I wasn't sure, but she was standing behind the counter and when she saw me, a huge grin broke out on her makeup-caked face. From across the room, she appeared almost decent, but up close it was impossible to not notice the chipped tooth she hadn't ever gotten fixed and the too-tight clothes that showed every last flaw of her figure.

What did she do, shop in the toddler section? I was so not in the mood for her today.

"Vaughn. Hey, gorgeous." She flashed me what she obviously thought was her flirty smile, but it came off as more of a sneer. "You're in early today. No action last night?"

I gave her a tight smile. "Lots of work to get done today. Large double espresso latte, please, and a coffee cake." I tossed a few bills on the counter and said, "Stash the rest in the tip jar."

"You're simply the sweetest," she gushed. "I bet you—"

Rudely, I turned my back to her and retreated into the lobby of the coffee shop. If I was forced to make conversation, this would turn ugly in two seconds flat. Today wasn't the day for that shit.

Norah huffed something that sounded like, "Rude-ass jerk," under her breath as she went to work on my giant cup of caffeine. When she was done, she called my name and cast me a dirty look. After placing my items on the counter, she stood there staring me down as I picked them up.

"Thanks," I said.

She scowled. Customer service be damned, I guess. "You know, if you're going to bring that attitude in here day in and day out, you can damn well find somewhere else to go for your morning coffee. Got it?"

Her outburst stopped me in my tracks. She'd never been anything short of bubbly and inviting before. This was a completely new side to Norah—that's what it said on her nametag. And it amused me.

"Did you hear me?" she barked.

I laughed and put another dollar in the tip jar. "Yep, loud and clear, boss." I raised the coffee and saluted her. "I'll adjust the attitude if you will."

"What? I'm always nice."

I nodded. "Yes. But maybe too nice. It is seven in the goddamned morning. Most of us are barely functional at this hour. If you could dial it back a few notches on the flirty scale, we'd get along much better."

"What's wrong, Vaughn?" she said dryly. "Too many women and not enough sleep?"

She was half right. "Just busy and not looking for anything other than my morning coffee, if you know what I mean."

Disappointment lined her face, but she smiled anyway. "Got it. Now apologize so we can be friends again."

"I think you got all the apology you need." I nodded to her tip jar and smiled as I walked out the front door.

I had a bike motor almost completely torn apart when the call came in. It was Mitch, my witch stepbrother. Holding the phone with my shoulder, I grabbed a rag and fruitlessly tried to scrape the grease off my fingers. "What do you need?"

"We've got a rogue witch we need you to track down. He or she appears to be summoning demons. Can you handle it?"

"I can track the witch, but don't expect me to bring him or her in. Not if they're knee-deep in demons."

"Sure, sure," Mitch said. "Just an ID. We'll do the rest."

"Okay, but I need about half an hour," I said, eyeing my torn and grease-smeared jeans.

"The witch appears to be wielding the spells now, so the sooner the better. I'll fax the information we have."

"Got it."

Mitch worked for the Witches' Council, and his job was to bring in witches that were on their radar for some reason or other. But he had to locate them first, and that was where I came in. I'm a tracker, a bounty hunter, for the supernatural crowd. I didn't have any real powers per se, only that I could sense magic when I was near someone wielding it. I was also really good at not being seen when I didn't want to be. That's what made me good at tracking. I could watch without being suspicious.

On my way out, I stopped by the boss's office. "Yo, Rick. I'm taking off for a few hours. I should have that bike done by tomorrow."

He waved me off without even looking up. He was relaxed in the extreme. It was one of the reasons I enjoyed working for him. As long as I got the job done, he didn't give a shit how much I worked or didn't work. In fact, the fewer hours I put in, the better, at least as far as his wallet was concerned.

My bike roared to life, and I took off for my apartment, where the recent memory of Matisse refused to disappear. The moment I walked in, I felt her presence with me again. "Son of a bitch," I muttered as I headed to the shower. "Get a grip, Paxton."

Ten minutes later, fresh from the shower and once again in clean clothes, I strode to the back of my apartment to my small makeshift office. The fax was waiting for me. The sheet was blank except for GPS coordinates. It would be the last known location, and that was all I was going to get.

Time to go. I bypassed my Indian and rounded the corner to my nondescript black SUV. After firing up the GPS, I took off. The mark was likely a young witch messing around with demon spells. It wasn't uncommon for teens to start dealing in darker magic. It was sort of like a drug for them. Forbidden and exciting. But it wasn't until my navigation system pointed me to the Coven Pointe neighborhood that I started to get a bad feeling.

The coven that lived there kept to themselves and rarely mixed with the rest of the witches of New Orleans. Not that I dealt with many of the other witches much. I'd met Beatrice Kelton a few times, the New Orleans coven leader. She ran a magic shop that sold some potions and healing herbs that even mundane people could use. If they knew what they were doing, that is. But I'd never had a reason to track one of her witches. That coven took care of their own.

The ones I was sent after were usually loners or ones who were just passing through. If this was a job dealing with the Coven Pointe witches, things could go south fast.

I drove down Opelousas and turned right on Sequin, heading for the levee. The location Mitch had sent over put the witch right on the edge of the Mississippi River. That was going to make fading into the background somewhat difficult. I'd just have to make do.

After parking my car on a side street, I shrugged into a dark jacket, pulled on a knitted cap, and grabbed my professional digital camera. It was used to take close-ups of my targets, but if anyone was paying attention to me, they'd likely assume I was a professional photographer. In New Orleans, photographers were a dime a dozen.

Damn it was cold. Up on the bike path that overlooked the Mississippi, the wind blew right through my jeans, nearly freezing my balls off. And to make matters worse, the entire waterfront was deserted. Not a single person populated the banks of the river. Shit. Had I misread the coordinates? I pulled the paper out of my back pocket and checked again. Nope. I must have missed the witch.

To make sure, I spent the next few minutes shooting pictures of the waterfront and then scanned the area once more. Nothing. Time to walk the streets. I tucked my camera into its pack and took off toward the neighborhood, but a tingle of magic caught my attention. It was coming from somewhere near the river.

Squinting, I moved to the edge of the ridge. There was no one. But damn, if that magic wasn't there. Then a flash of light that had me shielding my eyes came out of thin air. On impulse, I pulled the camera back out and set it on rapid fire. Whatever was going on, I needed to capture it.

Chapter 7

Matisse

Chessa pushed me behind her as the shadow morphed into solid form. "Go back to our world," she ordered.

"You want me to leave you here?" I asked, incredulity filling my tone. "Are you nuts?"

"Mati, you have—"

The demon charged out of the portal, his face contorted in rage. His red-tinted eyes narrowed at Chessa before he dismissed her and lunged, grabbing for me.

I jumped back, calling my magic to my fingertips. Sparks erupted, creating tiny lightning bolts of energy that fed into the ground.

"No!" Chessa's voice boomed in the darkness as she hurled an impressive fireball at the demon. But he only opened his mouth and caught it, swallowing it whole.

"Holy shit." Adrenaline fueled my magic, making the electricity come in stronger bursts. An electric barrier of pure energy formed around me, shielding me. And when the demon lashed out, connecting with the current, he yanked his gnarled hand back and screamed in obvious pain.

Chessa backed off, keeping a close eye on the demon, but I could see brilliant white power building around her in a fog.

"Who are you to knock at the door of Hell and deign to fight me?" Undeterred, the demon inched forward, advancing on me. "Your soul is worthless to me." He sniffed. "Dirty, foul sex witch. You're destined to spend the rest of your days trapped in stone for your sins."

My eyes widened in surprise at his outburst. Demons had a problem with sex witches? Was he kidding me? Demons? Then I met his evil glare with one of my own. "And you're destined to spend the rest of your days as ash, you evil soul-sucking bastard."

Focusing on the rage-induced power streaming from my fingers, I lifted my arms and threw everything I had at him. But all he did was raise a hand and let it all stream into him as if he was feeding off me.

I gasped, suddenly feeling more vulnerable than I ever had before. A moment ago, my power had scorched him. Now it did nothing to stop this demon. And he'd swallowed Chessa's fireball. She was right. I had to get out of there. But I couldn't leave her. And what about the demon? We'd called one up. If we left now, who knew where he'd end up?

"*Reverto!*" Chessa cried and flung a bolt of light at the demon. Again, he opened his mouth to welcome the magic, but instead of swallowing it down, the magic grew into a giant ball in his mouth. He stumbled back, writhing and choking on the electric energy.

Chessa grabbed my hand and squeezed as we both watched in fascinated horror.

"What's happening?" I asked, a tremor in my voice.

"I recalled the magic I threw at him earlier. Now it's mixing and if I did the spell right—"

The demon's eyes bulged and then a loud boom sounded as his head exploded, sending demon guts flying. We both ducked, but scaly flesh still landed on my arm.

"Oh, gross." My stomach rolled, and I struggled to hold back a gag.

The horrified look on Chessa's face told me she was doing the same thing.

The demon's body was lying on the ground twitching, no head in sight. Then as we backed away, the body combusted into ash.

"Whoa," I said, releasing Chessa's hand. Had my sister really just blown up a demon?

"Disgusting." She wiped dust off her white blouse and wrinkled her nose. "We better go."

"Yeah." I could barely breathe. Everything about what just happened was too horrifying.

"But we need to reappear in another spot. Preferably in a coven circle. If any more demons are coming, they'll follow. It'll be harder for them to burst through a properly sealed circle."

Harder but not impossible. I suppressed a shudder. "Okay." I could use our coven's circle, but it was in the middle of the Pointe and far too exposed, so I opted to borrow the New Orleans coven's circle. Theirs was shielded by a grove of oak trees. Aunt Dayla would approve. She'd been at war with their coven leader for years. Using their circle would be a bonus to her. Not that I had any issue with them. I just didn't want to explain to the rest of the coven what Chessa and I had been up to.

Chessa could maneuver through the shadows, but she didn't know them as well as I did, so I grabbed her hand again and focused on the circle, which wasn't too far from my college campus. It was on the other side of the river and we had no way to get home, but we'd figure it out.

The shadows started to fade, and my vision blurred with a hazy reality of green. When everything came back into focus, we were standing exactly where I'd willed us to go—smack-dab in the middle of the New Orleans' coven circle. Large oaks surrounded the clearing. The grass was pale green with patches of brown dead spots. No one was around.

The first thing I did was stop, drop, and roll to scrape away the demon remnants. Chessa stared at me, disgusted. I didn't care. The guts had to go, and what didn't come off easily, I rubbed on the patches of green grass. "You're crazy if you think I'm walking around with demon guts clinging to me."

She shook her head and waved a hand. Shimmering light spun around us both, and when it disappeared with a pop, we were both in fresh clothes, no guts in sight.

"Well that was… freaking awesome." I climbed to my feet. "How long have you been holding that spell back?"

She gave me a noncommittal shrug. "I try not to show off when it isn't necessary. But you're right. There was no way I was going anywhere in those clothes." She slipped her arm through mine. "Come on. I'll walk you to class. I hear you have a test to take."

We were only blocks from the university, but I wasn't exactly prepared. I frowned and glanced at my watch. Forty minutes until class started. "My notes and supplies are at home."

"Oh, no problem." She snapped her fingers, and my backpack appeared from thin air.

"What? I mean…?" Jeez. When had she become Ms. Super Powerful? I rummaged through the backpack and found everything I needed. "How did you do that?"

She grinned. "Being head angel in charge has its perks."

———

Vaughn

The rapid click of the shutter filled my senses as I focused on the bright magic pulsing on the banks of the Mississippi. I couldn't see anything but light and hoped the camera picked up something of use.

"What's that?" a male voice asked from behind me.

Fuck. Where'd he come from? My heart rate sped up with the surprise intrusion, and I took a deep breath as I turned around.

An older gentlemen dressed in a velour jogging suit squinted at the now fading light.

I shrugged and took a few more pictures. "No idea. Alien activity?"

"Government testing. Or radioactive contamination." The man chuckled and saluted me as he continued on down the path.

"Riiight." I turned back to the light, only to find it was completely gone and so was the magic. "Shit!"

I glanced over at the man. Had he been part of it? Been a distraction? It was possible. But that didn't explain where the magic had come from. Frustrated, I packed my camera back in its case and took off to search the neighborhood. I spent the next hour scouring the streets, but it was virtually useless. Too many witches lived there. I sensed magic in at least a dozen homes. There was no way to know if the one who'd been casting on the riverfront was in one of the houses now.

Frustrated, I climbed back into my SUV and headed home. Maybe I'd find something on the camera.

Back home in the Garden District, I called the shop to let the boss know I wouldn't be in until the next day.

"Whatever, man," Rick said. "Have fun with the lady."

"What lady?" I plugged my camera's memory card into the computer.

"The one who came looking for you. I though that's why you took off for the day."

Matisse? Had she stopped by the shop? How had she known where to find me? "What did she say?"

"Nothing. She was just looking for you. When you weren't here, she left. Real looker, too. Nice score, man."

For some reason his words pissed me off. They shouldn't, but they did. I didn't like thinking about the old perv ogling her. "Yeah. All right. See you tomorrow."

I sat at my desk, irritated at Mitch for sending me on a run that made me miss a visit from Mati. And if I didn't find the witch he was after, I wouldn't get paid at all. *Shit. Get your head in the game, asshole.* After a trip into the kitchen for a cup of coffee, I carried my mug back to the computer and got to work.

Chapter 8

Matisse

The test did not go well. I spent half the hour trying to block the demon out of my mind. But I just kept seeing him explode over and over again. The spreadsheet I was supposed to be filling in was just a sea of numbers. Who gave a shit about accounting when a demon had tried to kill me less than an hour ago?

Five minutes before class ended, I saved my file and clicked out of the program. No doubt I'd failed. I'd just sealed my fate. I'd have to retake the class for sure.

Outside in the hall I avoided Brandon, who was talking to one of his frat friends, and slipped out of the building. With my head down, I headed straight for Saint Charles. Once there, I hopped on the streetcar and settled in the back. I'm not sure I even knew where I intended to go until I jumped off near the Garden District. There was only one reason I'd ended up there.

Vaughn. Nervous energy skittered through me. What was I doing?

At least I had an excuse. With single-minded determination, I headed straight down Sixth Street until I was standing in front of the white Victorian. My breath caught in my throat. The light shining from his front windows told me everything I needed to know. He was home.

I could always leave after I got my keys, right? Yeah, that's what I'd come for. I scoffed at myself. Who was I kidding? After the day I had, all I wanted to do was lose myself in someone and recharge. I took a deep breath and went for it.

My knuckles hit the wood door in three solid raps.

Footsteps sounded from inside.

I glanced around and seriously considered darting behind a large water oak, but the door swung open before I could move, and there he was in his dark jeans, a long-sleeved shirt, and socks. He looked so relaxed. And even more inviting than he had the night before. My insides melted.

"Hey." He leaned against the doorframe and gave me a smug smile.

Cocky bastard. I raised one eyebrow as I eyed his overconfident stance. "Whatever you're thinking, you're wrong."

He laughed. "You sure about that?"

"Yes."

He stepped back and waved an arm, gesturing for me to come in. "It's pretty chilly out there. You're welcome to warm up in here."

I stepped over the threshold and eyed my keys, which were lying near a side table. There really was no reason for me to stay. Except not even a demon could've dragged me away from him right then. The sexual attraction I'd felt last night seemed to intensify to magnified proportions. I couldn't explain the phenomenon, and after the day I'd had, I didn't even want to.

Vaughn clasped my hand and tugged me through his shotgun-style apartment, all the way into the kitchen.

"Coffee?" he asked.

I nodded, leaning against the counter.

He filled a cup and placed it near me with a bottle of creamer and a bowl of sugar. As I doctored the coffee he said, "I'm glad you were able to track me down."

"Excuse me?" I took a small sip of the coffee and met his gaze.

"Rick said you came by the shop earlier."

"Rick?" I frowned. "Your shop? I don't even know where you work."

He crossed his arms over his chest. A wrinkle creased his brow and he mirrored my frown. "You didn't come by to see me today?"

"No." I chuckled. "I'm not a stalker."

"Really?" His lips twitched. "But you're here now."

"I left my keys. I came to pick them up." I couldn't let him think I was one of those weird, clingy girls who thought one night in the sack meant some sort of relationship. Hell no. We barely knew each other.

His face turned stormy, and I had to fight back a laugh. He wanted me here. And it didn't appear to be some misguided ego boost either. I mean, seriously. He clearly wasn't lacking in self-confidence.

"I see. So does that mean your friend is waiting for you?"

"What friend?"

He took a step closer, his eyes burning into me. "The one who picked you up in the middle of the night last night."

Oh. Right. "Um, no. I took the streetcar."

That smoldering gaze dipped to my mouth.

I took my time, wetting my lips just to see what he would do.

His right arm flexed, but to my disappointment, he raised his gaze and took a step back. Then he stuffed his hands in his pockets. It was almost as if he were forcing himself to not touch me. Damn. There was that disappointment again. I took another long sip of my coffee.

Finally he asked, "Are you hungry?"

What a loaded question. Hell yes I was. But not really for food. "What did you have in mind?"

He took the coffee cup from me. "There's a French restaurant on Magazine."

"Yeah, sure, I could eat." Because if I didn't go, I'd be ripping his clothes off in two minutes flat. Desperation didn't look good on me.

His shoulders relaxed and some of the tension eased from his face. "Good. It's been a busy day. I haven't eaten."

He took off through his apartment, and I followed. We had to pass through his bedroom on our way out, but when we got there, he sat on the edge of his bed. Memories of what we'd done the night before filled my head. I couldn't stop the heat from burning my cheeks. I hadn't been in this position before. How was I supposed to act? Did dinner mean he expected a repeat of the night before? And what would I do if he didn't? Seduce him anyway?

Once he had his shoes on, he stood and placed a hand on the small of my back. "Ready?"

"Sure." His touch was so comfortable and oddly familiar it put me at ease. And suddenly, I wanted more than the life I'd been leading. I wanted someone to drop in on. Someone I cared about enough to spend more than one night with. Brandon was a possibility. He was a nice guy, but this natural chemistry that I had with Vaughn was missing. We'd bore each other before too long. I vowed right then and there to enjoy myself while I was with Vaughn. Consequences be damned. Was it so terrible to care about someone?

"So," I said. "You had a mystery woman come by your shop. Who do you think it could be?" The obvious answer was some other one-night stand who couldn't seem to stay away either. But I was comforted by the fact that he'd immediately assumed the person had been me. Plus he'd clearly been pleased to see me.

"I have no idea." He ran a hand through his dark hair. It fell in short waves over his forehead.

I had to stop myself from brushing it out of his eyes. "Ah, secret admirer. Exciting."

"Or irritating." He laughed.

I gave him a mock look of horror as we turned onto Magazine Street. "What? You don't like random women just showing up out of the blue?"

His eyes gleamed with mischief. "It depends on the woman."

Oh, I could play this game. Warmth spread through my belly with the knowledge he was going to enjoy this just as much as I was. "So you're into stalkers then? You like being chased, rather than do the chasing? Seems about right considering how things got started last night."

"Ha!" His body shook with mild laughter. "I seem to recall someone doing her best to torment me and then spending her time fawning over some Ken doll. If I hadn't taken your not-so-subtle bait, I'm pretty sure I'd have ended up alone last night."

It was my turn to scoff. "Right. Alone. That seems likely."

The humor vanished from his face and he turned serious eyes on me. "You'd be surprised." But before I could question him, heat filled his eyes again and he added, "At least last night anyway. After that body shot, I had to find out what was under that skirt."

My body had such a visceral response to the memories of the night before, I bit my lip to keep from moaning right there on the street. Goddess, he was winning again! I couldn't have that. I brushed my fingers down the inside of his arm. "And did you like what you saw?"

He stopped in the middle of the block, wrapping his fingers around mine.

"I thought we were getting dinner," I said with a teasing smile.

He stared at me, his smoldering gaze searing me from the inside out. "You should know I spent most of the day replaying the image of you undressing for me. I think it's safe to say I liked what I saw."

Well, that was... hot. I didn't have a snappy comeback. My mind was too busy recalling last night's events.

"If you keep looking at me like that, we're not going to make it to dinner." Vaughn took a step closer and clasped one hand around my neck as he caressed my jaw with his thumb.

I cleared my throat. "I thought you were hungry."

"That's a fair assessment." His husky voice was low and full of promise.

Excitement shot through my core. How fast could we get back to his apartment? His fingers were tracing my neck, sending shivers of pleasure from the exact spot he'd bit down on twice the night before. I knew there was a small mark there from his love bites and wondered if he knew it, too. "Kiss me," I said, my voice just as husky as his.

His hand slipped lower, but my neck continued to tingle as he leaned in and granted my request. His kiss was hungry, sinfully demanding in the way he pulled me closer and lifted me onto my toes as he pulled me up to meet him. I matched his intensity, catching his lower lip between my teeth. Who needed food with this guy around?

He let out a small groan and tightened his arms around me. We were lost, overtaken as the world around us slipped away.

That is, until the whooping started from a small group of tourists across the street, followed by the squeal of brakes from a car sliding to a stop mere feet from where we stood.

"Son of a bitch!" Vaughn cried and yanked me out of the way, causing me to stumble and fall on the uneven sidewalk.

"Dude! What the fuck?" an angry male voice shouted from the car.

Vaughn ignored him and helped me stand.

Pain pulsed through my knee and when I went to inspect it, I found torn jeans and blood. "Ouch," I yelped as I grazed my fingers over the wound.

"Vaughn!" the man yelled again, the anger in his voice intensifying. "What the hell are you doing?"

"Making sure you don't kill my date, you asshole." Vaughn's tone was laced with a dangerous edge. "What's your problem?"

The dark-haired man in his early thirties jumped from the car and slammed the door. "I've been waiting for your phone call. Dude. You have a job to do."

"I'm working on it." Vaughn tucked me to his side, placing a protective arm around my shoulders. "When I have something for you, I'll be in touch."

The man's nostrils flared in disgust. "You and your skanks. Man, that dick of yours is going to get someone killed one of these days."

"What did you just call me?" I pulled away from Vaughn's grasp, power pooling in my palms.

He finally gave me a long look and recognition dawned as his gaze landed on my hands. "Are you helping him?" He spun and glared at Vaughn. "What are you doing with a witch?"

"Mitch, get the fuck out of here before I beat the shit out of you." Vaughn took a menacing step forward. "And don't ever talk to her like that again. Show some goddamned respect for once in your life."

I tamped my magic down and took a step back. "Clearly you two have something to work out. I think I'll be on my way."

Vaughn clasped his hand over my wrist. "No. We don't. And if he has any sense at all, he'll get back in his rust bucket and leave."

I was startled at his possessive grip and panic flashed through me. But not because of the obvious dominance. Oh no. Because I liked it. When had anyone of the opposite sex had the balls to take charge in my life? Never. They were too busy doing whatever I said in the hope they'd get laid later.

Mitch scowled. "We don't have time for this. Things are getting… out of control."

"Not my problem," Vaughn said through clenched teeth. A muscle in his neck pulsed.

Mitch gave me one last look of disdain and then pursed his lips in a flat line before saying, "Don't say I didn't warn you." Then he climbed back into his circa-1990s Toyota and sped off down the street again.

We stood on the sidewalk staring at each other for a moment. I wasn't sure what to say.

"Well. That was… uncalled for." Vaughn held his hand out. "Are you still up for some food? And maybe I can explain what that was about?"

As attracted as I was to him, I wasn't going to sign up for a relationship that came with a generous helping of the criminally insane. No thank you. I was about to shake my head no when he let out a frustrated sigh. "He's my stepbrother, otherwise I would've cut ties with him years ago. It's hard to ditch family."

Now that was something I could understand. Against my better judgment, I took his still-outstretched hand. "Dinner sounds great."

Chapter 9

Vaughn

I led Matisse into the neighborhood corner bistro. Vale, the maître d' who happened to be a good friend of mine, was on the phone and waved us into the dining room. I chose a secluded table in the back.

A waitress appeared, handed us menus, and took our drink orders. Abita Turbodog for me and a sweet tea for Matisse.

She sat back in her chair. "So…"

I scanned the menu, avoiding her gaze. There was no need. I always ordered the same thing, but I needed a moment to collect my thoughts. How much should I tell her? Not that I was a bounty hunter. Not yet. I had a cover to maintain. But I could explain about Mitch.

"Good evening." The tall platinum-blond waitress pulled out a pen and a faux-leather tablet. "Would you like to hear the specials?"

Matisse flashed the waitress a sweet smile that made me want to reach out and caress her lips. "Sure."

Dude, get a grip.

The waitress rattled off four or five things, none of which I retained. I was too busy watching my date. *Date.* That's the second time I'd used that term in the last ten minutes. What would she say to that?

"And for you, sir?" the waitress prompted.

Right. Matisse had just ordered one of the specials. "Shrimp and grits, please."

"Excellent choice." The waitress wandered off once again.

Matisse cleared her throat. "You were going to fill me in on what happened back there?"

Better to just start at the beginning. "I already told you Mitch is my stepbrother. He's also a witch."

"It's hard to believe you two are related." She seemed more interested in my family history than the fact that he was a witch. Though, she'd probably already sensed his magic anyway.

"We don't really get along all that well."

Her eyes lit up as she laughed. She seemed so fresh and relaxed. It was even more alluring than the natural attraction that was running rampant between us. "That seemed fairly obvious."

I grinned sheepishly. "I guess so. Anyway, I do contract work for the, ah, company he works for, and I gather he's under a lot of pressure from his bosses." I shrugged. "Apparently I'm not moving fast enough for them. But since I only get paid when I deliver, it's not like they can fire me or anything."

She raised a skeptical eyebrow. "And yet you're here with me instead of working on the project?"

"I've been working on it all day." I ignored the nagging doubt in my mind that I should be doing something more to find the rogue witch. But since I didn't have anything else to go on at present, it wasn't like I'd just dropped the job. Besides, I was right where I wanted to be. "There isn't much more I can do today anyway."

"Gotcha."

Our waitress brought our drinks and set them down hard enough that Matisse's tea sloshed onto the table. The waitress's friendly demeanor had vanished, replaced by a scowl. She didn't even apologize for spilling a third of the liquid.

We watched her stalk away. Once she disappeared into the kitchen, Matisse turned her attention to me. "Looks like someone's having a bad day."

"I guess so." I handed her an extra napkin as she mopped up the tea.

When she was done, I was completely captivated as she wrapped her lips around the straw. She had to have felt the heat rippling from me because she lifted her gaze to mine and sent me her seductive smile. The same one that had lured me in so well the night before.

I placed my elbows on the table and leaned in. "Matisse?"

Her smile widened as she sat back, crossing her arms over her chest. She knew exactly what she was doing. "Yes?"

"Come here," I commanded.

She didn't move. Her eyes never wavered from mine. And for a minute, I was certain she wasn't going to give me what I wanted. But then she placed her hands flat on the table, leaned in, and brought her lips inches from mine. "What exactly is it you want, Mr. Paxton?"

"I think you know the answer to that." I inched closer, stopping just shy of pressing my lips to hers, tormenting both of us. I wanted her lips on me. Wanted to throw her down on the table and rip her clothes off.

Her breath caught. Was the witch reading my mind? Goddamn, I hoped so. The tip of her tongue glided over her lower lip as she stared at my mouth. I felt my lips curl into a self-satisfied smile.

But she didn't seem to notice. Or if she did, she didn't give a damn, because she inched forward and pressed her lips to mine, her hot tongue slipping into my mouth, tasting and exploring at her will.

I let my eyes close and breathed in her light honeysuckle scent. It was so subtle and not at all exotic, but it was intoxicating and made me want to taste every inch of her.

Bam!

The table shook as dishes crashed onto the surface. Matisse and I jerked apart to find our waitress with wild, red-tinged eyes glaring at us. Our plates had been slammed onto the edge of the table with most of the food splattered on the floor.

Matisse jumped up. "What—"

The waitress growled, and her form morphed into a gnarled, wrinkled version of herself as her jaw elongated and her nails grew to pointed daggers on her fingertips.

"Jesus!" I sprang out of my chair, but the demon reached out, slicing through Matisse's sweater. Streaks of blood seeped through the white cotton.

"Son of a... Fuck!" I reached for her, but before I could intervene, Matisse let out a roar of pain. Magic sprang from her raised hands, and a flash of light encircled the demon, momentarily trapping her.

"You're mine, dirty witch." The demon spat green-tinged mucus at Matisse's feet. She jumped back just in time before the mucus exploded into a puff of smoke.

Holy shit. Exploding mucus. I glanced around. Where was everyone else in the restaurant? The place was eerily empty except for the three of us. Without any idea of how to battle the magical creature, I grabbed a chair and swung.

My arms reverberated with the massive impact. The demon fell to her knees, but as she went down, red lightning shot from her mouth and caught Matisse's leg. Matisse went rigid and convulsed in place as the demon cackled with victory.

Protective rage filled every inch of my being. My hands tightened around the solid wood chair, and with a force I hadn't known I'd possessed, I swung. The makeshift weapon splintered against the side of the demon's head. The demon sat there, stunned, as the chair broke apart around her.

"Dammit!" With one hand I grabbed a broken table leg and fisted a fallen steak knife with the other.

Matisse had slid to the floor and was clutching her leg as her body trembled with shock. The utter pain on her face cut me to the core. But there was no time to waste, because the demon had her sights on me now and was on her feet, coming straight for me.

"Come on!" I taunted, wielding the knife and crude wooden stake as if I'd been training for this my entire life. The defensive stance seemed so completely natural it was unexplainable. I'd taken a few boxing lessons, but nothing that would explain why I seemed to be trained in combat.

The demon reached both arms out, grabbing for my head, but I swung my left arm, cutting the blow off with the wooden stake and followed immediately with a strike of the knife. The blade hit home in the demon's shoulder. She recoiled, hissing what appeared to be steam. But I didn't stop. The demon had gone after Matisse. She had to be destroyed.

I surged forward on the offensive and just when I was about to drive the stake in the demon's chest, she turned, spraying me with that steam.

"Fuck!" It burned like hell, almost as if I'd been pepper-sprayed. Tears flooded my eyes, and I stumbled back, blinded. "Son of a bitch," I cried, my arms flailing, trying to connect with any part of the demon. But there was nothing but air.

"You opened the gates," the demon said in a sinister tone.

What the hell did that mean?

"And you killed my mate, dirty witch." Another snarl escaped the demon. "It's time to pay. Your life for his."

Matisse's strong voice filled the room. "No! By my word to the Goddess, I command you back to Hell!"

Thunder rumbled, shaking the furniture as the dishes rattled on the tables. Then I heard a boom, followed by what sounded like an electric sizzle.

I wiped at my burning eyes and tried to peer through the blur. A fuzzy outline appeared before me.

"Vaughn?" Matisse's voice was soft, full of concern.

"I'm fine," I said, scooting back, not wanting to be coddled. "I need water."

There was a slight rustling and the clink of glass against what must be a pitcher of some sort. Then her delicate hand wrapped around my wrist as she pressed a cold glass into my palm. "Here."

"Thanks." Still mostly blind, I fished the ice out of the glass. Then I forced my eyes open and dumped the water over my irritated eyes. "Holy fucking shit!" That burned. Blinking rapidly, I poured more water over my face, and after what seemed like hours, though it was likely only a few minutes, the restaurant came back into view.

"Welcome back," Matisse said as I finally focused on her. She'd ripped apart one of the linen tablecloths and bandaged her leg. Funny how I hadn't heard that while I'd been cleansing my eyes. "You okay?"

"I'll be fine."

We were both sitting on the painted concrete floor as the staff slowly started to emerge from the back.

"Where's the new waitress?" one of them asked.

Neither of us answered. But only Matisse knew for sure where the demon had gone.

The front door blasted open, and two men wearing official-looking black jackets and odd badges burst through. They did a sweep of the restaurant. When they came up empty, they headed straight for us.

I climbed to my feet and held a hand out to Matisse. There were many questions for her to answer, but I'd be damned if I made her do it alone. She cast me a grateful look and struggled to get to her feet due to her injured leg. I wrapped my arm around her, giving her the support she needed to stand upright.

The taller official glanced over his shoulder at the restaurant workers, who were staring at us. Turning back to us, he jerked his head toward the door. "I think we should talk outside."

"Fine." I helped Matisse navigate the disaster created by the struggle. With each wince and hiss that escaped her sweet lips, a piece of me hardened. Had she really opened the gates of Hell? Was she the witch I'd been looking for? I didn't want to believe it. But the more I tried to explain the demon's words away, the more convinced I was that she was the rogue witch. Why else would a demon come after her in broad daylight?

Once outside, the official took a rundown of exactly what had happened in the restaurant, confirmed Matisse was a witch and that I wasn't, and then they thanked us and left.

"Who the hell was that?" I asked her. They weren't with the NOLA PD. Or any other government law enforcement.

She stared at her feet.

"Matisse?" I kept my tone low and as even as possible. We'd had enough conflict for one day.

"Can we go back to your apartment?" she asked, still avoiding my gaze.

"Sure."

At first the walk was slow and tedious, but with each step, Matisse seemed to be getting stronger. By the time we reached my apartment, she was barely even limping.

"Did you cast a spell?" I eyed her as I unlocked the door. "Or do you have super healing capabilities?"

That got a smile out of her. "It's a spell. Though it did take a lot out of me. I might be walking better, but I still feel like shit."

I would've never guessed. Besides looking rumpled, she was as gorgeous as ever. But now wasn't the time to dwell on that. I held the door open for her. She stood in my entry hall, fidgeting. Fidgeting? She'd just beaten down a demon and here she was, consumed by nerves. Was it the fact we were alone in my apartment once more or the fact that she'd just banished a demon? I was hoping for the former.

Chapter 10

Matisse

How did a girl explain to a guy she was dangerously attracted to that she was a sex witch, related to the high angel, and was using him for sex in order to close the portal to Hell? Yeah. No. Maybe the demon-portal thing was enough.

I sat on Vaughn's leather couch and waited for him to return. He'd disappeared into the kitchen after saying something about bottled water. But when he took more than a few minutes to return, I got up and hovered near the door.

"I've got it taken care of." Vaughn had his back turned to me as he talked into his iPhone. "Yes. She's here… No. Don't come over. Fuck, dude. I told you I'm handling it." He pulled the phone away from his ear, shook his head, and hit End before tossing it on the counter with enough force that it bounced a couple of times.

"Your brother?" I asked, leaning against the doorframe.

He flinched and turned in my direction, clearly startled.

"Sorry. Didn't mean to eavesdrop. I'm just a little thirsty." I nodded toward the bottled water sitting on the counter.

"Right." He grabbed both bottles and shuffled me out of the room.

We sat on his couch in silence as he studied me with a mix of curiosity and confusion. I took one of the waters and watched him struggle with himself while I drank a quarter of it.

Finally he squared his shoulders, looked me straight in the eye, and asked, "Are you a witch who deals with demons?"

I sputtered mid-sip. "What?"

"The demon." He leaned in, scrutinizing me. "She said you opened the portal and destroyed her mate. Is this just another normal day for you?"

The way he asked the question 'Is this just another normal day for you' sounded very much like an accusation. Irritated, I sat back. "No. I don't play around with demons. What the hell kind of question is that?"

He got to his feet but kept his gaze fixed on me. "Did you try to open a portal today?"

His no-nonsense questioning was seriously starting to piss me off. Never mind that he was almost on target. The implied accusation was uncalled for. He could've asked me without making me feel like a criminal.

I stood, ignoring the pain shooting down my leg. The wound had healed, but it would be sore for a while. I placed my hands on my hips and stared back at him with all the judgment he was laying at my feet. "What about you? How exactly do you know about demon portals?"

"You didn't answer my question."

"And you didn't answer mine." His brother was a witch. It wasn't unfeasible that he would be knowledgeable about demons, but couldn't he just ask what I knew about the demon without putting me on trial? The thought made my blood boil.

"Fine." He stalked over to me and gestured for me to sit.

I held my ground.

He shook his head in exasperation and then sat across from me on his coffee table, resting his elbows on his knees. "Stand all night if you want to, but I'm fairly certain you're still recovering. It's probably better if you rest."

I glanced at my leg and grimaced when I realized it was trembling slightly. Damn him for being right. Reluctantly, I sat back on the couch.

His lips twitched and a smug smile broke out on his face. I glared. The smile vanished, but the gleam in his eye didn't. Bastard.

"Tell me what you really do for your brother," I demanded.

"You first."

We had a stare-off to end all stare-offs that was only broken by the incessant ringing of his phone.

"You should probably get that," I said and leaned back into the couch.

"It's Mitch."

"So?"

He gave me a pointed look. "He wants answers I can't give him."

I sat straight up, holding back a wince from the demon slashes on my ribs. Damn, that hurt. "I knew you were asking these questions for him." But then a realization settled over me. He'd said his brother was a contractor for someone. As a witch, that likely meant one organization. The Witches' Council. "Wait. Am I being investigated?"

"Yes."

"No way!" I stood again and winced when another dart of pain shot down my thigh. Grabbing it, I stifled a whimper.

A second later Vaughn was by my side, giving me a shoulder to lean on. "Come on. You need to relax."

Because the throb in my leg wasn't going away and he'd dropped the interrogator act to help me, I let him lead me into the next room and then into his bedroom. I came to an abrupt stop the moment we stepped through the door. What we'd done the night before was too fresh in my mind. We'd been two strangers using each other. Tonight we were something else. Friends? Enemies? Certainly not lovers. And being there was making it hard for me to breathe.

"What's wrong?" he asked, concern lacing his tone.

I shook my head, totally out of my element. "Uh, nothing. What are we doing in here?"

"You need to lie down and the bed is a thousand times more comfortable than that old couch." He tugged on my hand. When I didn't budge, he swept me up in his arms, and despite my protest, he carried me to the bed and gently laid me on top of his comforter.

The gesture was far too considerate and sweet for me to continue to be pissed at him. He was an enigma. One moment he was acting the insensitive a-hole and the next he was taking care of me even when I was being stubborn.

My heart fluttered. Crap on toast. This was going to get messy.

Vaughn walked around to the other side of the bed and sat next to me, leaning against his headboard.

"Okay. I'll talk if you will," I said somewhat reluctantly. The work I did for Chessa was classified, but if I was being investigated by the Witches' Council, it was better they knew I was working from orders. Not to mention Vaughn had been caught up in a demon fight. If there were any more coming after me tonight, he deserved to know he was in danger.

"Deal."

We stared at each other, both of us obviously expecting the other to go first.

I chuckled. "All right. No, I wasn't trying to open a portal. I was trying to seal one. And before you go thinking that's the sort of thing I do for fun, it isn't. I work for the high angel and that particular task is something she's had me working on. I do not get off on dealing with demons."

"The high angel?" He raised a curious eyebrow. "Isn't it a little unusual for a college student to be working for the Angel Council?"

"Yes. It would be." It sounded so absurd when he put it like that. "Except the high angel is my sister and this isn't exactly sanctioned by the Angel Council." Oh, oops! I bit down on my tongue, realizing I probably shouldn't have added that last part.

"Really? So why is she so bent on sealing it up?" He seemed curious, not judgmental this time, which I appreciated. But I was still skeptical. He hadn't told me anything yet. Not that Chessa's reason was top secret or anything. "An angel she was close to was taken through the portal and fell. Chessa will do anything to seal it up."

"I see." He rubbed his five-o'clock shadow. I wanted to reach out and run my fingers over the stubble, but I refrained. Now wasn't the time. "That's rough."

His voice was so full of compassion that I had a sudden change of heart. Now seemed like the perfect time. I reached over and lightly trailed the back of my fingers down his cheek to his jawline. We both froze, staring at each other for an intense moment.

When I dropped my hand, he cleared his throat. "Can't say I blame her. Is that what you were doing today on the west bank? In the Pointe, right? Near the river?"

I turned to watch him. "How did you know that?"

He shrugged. "That's what I do. I'm a bounty hunter—"

"What?" My spine went completely rigid and then I rolled off the bed, fuming. "Is that why you took me home last night?"

"Huh?" He looked up at me in confusion. "I didn't... Oh shit. No, no. That's not at all what happened." He leaped off the bed and landed next to me. "Please. Sit back down and I'll start at the beginning. I swear, I absolutely had no idea who you were last night when I brought you home. You were just too damn sexy to pass up. And that's God's honest truth."

Too damn sexy. Well, I could live with that, I guess. Most men thought that about me anyway. It was the sex magic. Still, I sat on the very edge of the bed, ready to bolt if I suspected he was lying. Though I had no reason to believe he was. Except for the fact he was a bounty hunter and apparently I was on his radar. And that sort of pissed me off, too. I mean, he was the one guy I'd liked well enough to see twice and he'd been hired to hunt me. Eff balls. "Okay. Start at the beginning."

"My brother is a witch, and he works for the Witches' Council, keeping an eye on unusual supernatural activity. I moonlight as a bounty hunter, tracking down leads for him and others who do his sort of work. I wasn't working on any case at all yesterday. I got the call to track you down today and the only information I had was GPS coordinates. But when I got there, for some reason I could sense you but not see you." He cast me a sidelong glance. "Why is that, by the way?"

My shadow-walking ability wasn't exactly a secret, but it wasn't public knowledge either. I wasn't sure how much of myself I wanted to reveal to this guy, especially if he was somehow working for the Witches' Council. They didn't really care for my particular coven. The old prudes weren't real tolerant of sex witches. I met his questioning glance. "How is it you knew I was there if you couldn't see me?"

He chuckled. "I knew you weren't going to let that pass. While I don't have any real magical abilities, I can sense when someone is using magic. And then there's this." He pulled his laptop from the nightstand and powered it up. After opening a file, pictures of the levee on the west bank filled the screen. In every single one of them was a brilliant flash of light on the deserted waterfront. It was the same spot Chessa and I had been standing when we'd stepped into the Shadow world. The pictures had to be me casting the spell to close the portal.

I met his curious stare. "You saw me?"

He nodded. "But I didn't know it was you."

"I had no idea my magic was visible while I was… Shit, you said you could sense me?"

That gleam was back and my stomach all but fell to my feet. Did that mean he'd known I was using some sort of magic to prime the pump, so to speak, at the club last night? Jeezus. How freakin' humiliating.

"Don't worry about it," he said quietly.

I swallowed, horrified. He'd known the whole time. "Worry about what?"

"About the magic you used last night. Whatever it was, it didn't make me do anything I didn't want to."

Now his expression was completely stoic. Could I trust him? I wanted to. There'd never been a member of the opposite sex I could talk to about these things. It was new and entirely too comfortable. I shrugged. "It's not much. A suggestion really. In order for it to work, the person has to be interested already. It's not like I can control someone's will."

"Just their willpower." He grinned.

There wasn't any of that previous judgment behind his words, and that made all the difference. I shook my head, suppressing a smile. "You could say that."

"At no point did I contemplate resisting. Does that make you feel better?"

I smirked. "I wasn't feeling bad about it."

He nodded. "I see. Well then, I guess we can move on."

"Okay." I shifted to stretch my sore leg. It was feeling better already. "Then tell me why the Council thinks I was opening a demon portal."

"Nope. Not until you tell me how come I couldn't see you. Do you have some sort of invisibility cloak à la Harry Potter or something?"

"Goddess, no. But that would be really cool." I clasped my hand over his arm and leaned in. "Can you imagine how useful that would be? Especially in your line of work?"

"Nice try, Matisse. But stop deflecting the question."

Damn him. I lifted my hands, palms up. "You can't blame a girl for trying. Still, you have to admit it would be a cool tool."

His body had relaxed as he leaned against his headboard and his face was set in a small smile. He was thoroughly enjoying this. And the realization made me warm all over. I wasn't sending any pheromones out into the atmosphere. In fact, if anything, I was trying to keep myself pretty guarded at the moment. I didn't really like exposing details about myself. And the fact that he was enjoying our time together made me ridiculously happy. Is this what it's like to be in a relationship?

The idea of being impossibly attracted to someone and being able to enjoy a good debate, to trust them with important matters, was terrifying. I'd never realized I wanted that before. But dammit if I didn't crave it now.

Something must have shifted in my expression, because he reached out and caressed my neck just below my ear. The action sent a small tremor through my tired body and made me want to curl up next to him with his arms around me.

Again, totally new territory for me. Sex witches usually weren't needy like that. Or were we? If we never got close to anyone, how would we know? Before I could act on my impulse, he pulled his hand away.

"If not a cloak, how does it work?" he asked, bringing me back to the conversation.

Oh hell. Might as well just get it all out there. What would it hurt if he knew anyway? "I'm a shadow walker."

He frowned. "A what?"

"There is a world between ours and Hell, where spirits sometimes get trapped. I can walk in that world. There's an open demon portal there. Chessa and I were trying to seal it so demons can't reach New Orleans anymore."

His gorgeous eyes widened as his expression morphed into one of awe. "That's a lofty goal. I take it it didn't work?"

I shook my head. "No. In fact, it brought attention to the portal and Chessa had to fight one of them off. It's not like we were looking for trouble. Chessa had to do what she did. She had no choice. It was either him or us."

He furrowed his brow, clearly thinking. "I wonder why the Council thought you were trying to summon a demon."

"I have no idea. I work for the Angel Council, not the Witches' Council. I can't even venture a guess as to what they were thinking. But I should let Chessa know we're on their radar. She should be able to clear everything up."

Vaughn got up from the bed. "I'll let Mitch know it's taken care of."

"No!" I lunged and grabbed his hand to stop him.

He gave me a stunned look.

I let go. "Sorry. It's just that I'd like Chessa to talk to the Council first before you involve anyone else. The stuff I just told you, it's confidential. If it gets out, I'm going to be in a heap of shit."

He appeared dubious, but after a moment, he nodded. "Sure."

"I'll pay whatever your bounty-hunting fee is so you're not out a job. Let me know how much and I'm sure Chessa will take care of it." I slipped my phone from my jeans and started punching in Chessa's private number. She'd banned me from even programming it. That's how private it was.

But Vaughn snatched the phone from my hand and stood over me, a stormy expression on his face.

"Hey!" I stared up at him, irritated. "Give me my phone back."

He shoved it in his pocket and shook his head. "Not until we get this straight."

"Get what straight?" I got to my feet, not at all pleased with the way he was standing over me.

He took a step closer, invading the last inches of my personal space. "Under no circumstances am I going to let you pay my bounty-hunting fee. Not only is that unethical, but it's offensive. I'm not here with you now because of the money. Got that?"

"I never—"

"I'm here because I want to spend time with the sexy witch who seduced the shit out of me last night and left me hungry for more."

"Well, that's flattering," I said with heavy sarcasm.

"You should be flattered." His voice was rough as his desire-filled eyes bored into me. "It takes someone special to catch my attention and keep it." He let out a low, ironic chuckle. "And don't be giving me that offended glare. You're exactly the same way. I can sense it all over you. The way you left all those men wanting you back at the club. The subtle magic you use to attract whoever catches your eye. And then the way you flee after you've gotten what you want. Don't for a minute stand there and act like what I said is any different from the way you operate. Because I can see right through you."

And even though my head said I should slap him and walk away, or at the very least tell him what a piece of shit he was for his crass assessment of me after knowing me for less than twenty-four hours, I did neither of those things. Because he was right. And the fact that he had called me on it only made me want him all the more.

"Matisse?" he said, dropping his gaze to my lips.

"Vaughn?" I breathed.

"It's going to be a while before you can make that phone call."

My pulse quickened and something fluttered in my stomach. "And why is that?" I managed to force out.

"Because, my gorgeous witch, I'm going to take you to bed now and make you ache with need until you beg me to make love to you."

Chapter 11

Matisse

Vaughn dipped his head and moved in to claim my lips. His words kept repeating in a loop in my head.

I'm going to take you to bed and make you ache with need.

I was already there. Just his words had ignited a passion so fierce, so lustful, that every part of me begged to be touched. My fingers curled into his shirt, fisting the fabric as our tongues met and tangled together.

The kiss was hot, full of pent-up tension, but the frenzy was offset by his slow, gentle caress of my neck. His fingers trailed lightly from the base of my skull down to my nape and circled the love bite he'd given me the night before. Once again as soon as he touched me there, electric heat shot from the mark straight to my center, causing me to gasp with the delightful sensation.

His chest rumbled with a light chuckle.

"What did you do to me?" I asked, my lips pressed against his.

He pulled away slightly to gaze into my eyes. "You've been marked."

But before I could ask what he meant, he lifted me off my feet and covered my mouth with his. I wrapped my legs around his waist as he carried me into his bathroom. Then the shower was on and he was peeling me out of my soiled clothes.

I stood there letting him do what he would, completely turned on by the intimacy of the moment. Every thought of the day's events flew out of my head as each garment was stripped from my body, followed by his gentle touch over my bare skin. It wasn't until his hand brushed over my neck and the tingling started again that I remembered what he'd said. Standing naked in his bathroom, I touched his hand, stopping his careful exploration. "What did you mean, I've been marked?"

His eyes focused on my neck and then he placed his fingers over the area, carefully tracing the faint bruise. "Only that I'd left a mark on you. It'll fade."

Why did I like the fact that he had marked me? The feminist in me wasn't amused. But the woman in me thought it was hot as hell. I hooked a finger in one of his belt loops and tugged him the last few inches toward me. And as I undid his belt, he bent his head to my neck and went to work on loving that spot on my neck. My knees turned to jelly as heat flooded my body. "Oh, that's nice."

I felt him smile against my skin, and with a gentle tug, I relieved him of his jeans and boxer briefs. Then I traced my hands over his abs, exploring every toned dip and ridge. Eff me. His body was outrageous. I could've spent all night just touching him. That is until he tugged his shirt off and pulled me into the hot stream of water. He turned me so I was standing in front of him and then he went to work on washing every part of my body. The warmth and slippery touch of his soapy fingers soothed me.

He took his time washing my back, my limbs, and even took care to massage my fingers. The total luxury of giving myself over to someone else was tantalizing, and for once, I didn't feel threatened by my own vulnerability. I loved it. Loved giving up the control and trusting this man to give me what I needed.

After carefully washing and conditioning my hair, he handed me the shower gel and stood before me, silently asking me to do the same for him. I was all too willing. My fingers were eager to touch, to explore, and to know all the ridges and angles of his tall frame. I took my time washing his hair, gratified when he tilted his head back with his eyes closed, clearly enjoying my touch. Once I was done, I grazed my fingers along the indent of his narrow waist, smiling when I reached around and ran my hand along the silky plane of his arousal.

A small, strangled moan escaped his lips as he grew harder under my touch.

Kissing his shoulder, I palmed him and slowly slid my hand up and down and then repeated the motion.

"Matisse," he said, placing his hand over mine to stop the torment.

I squeezed gently, sending a small shiver through him. "Yes, Vaughn?"

"Maybe it's better for both of us if we put the pause button on that activity for a moment." He turned and flattened his hands against the tile, trapping me between him and the wall. "Because there's a lot more I have planned before this evening is over."

I raised my hands in surrender. "I'm all yours."

His dark eyes sparked with intensity, and I bit my lip as I realized I'd just given up all control. But it was so freeing and so damned alluring that I stood there, waiting for him to make another move.

He dipped his head, gently kissing one of my fingers, and curled his right hand around my left. The gesture was so sweet and tender it nearly brought tears to my eyes. But then he slipped another one of my fingers into his mouth and sucked, sending a bolt of lightning that heated me from the inside out. A moan of pleasure tore from the back of my throat.

His low chuckle vibrated over my fingers, and the thought of his mouth on other more sensitive places made my insides churn with anticipation.

"More," I said, arching so my nipple was inches from his lips.

He didn't disappoint. He turned his head and clasped his teeth around my already pebbled peak and moved his hand down to my hip, possessively digging his fingers into my flesh.

"Yes," I whispered.

That tiny word, yes, was like a dam bursting, and his mouth was suddenly everywhere, kissing and biting my flesh until my breasts were aching and heavy. The sensations were breathtaking in a way that left me unable to do anything except lean against the cool tile and let him devour me.

Before long, he shifted and kissed his way down my stomach, stopping just before his tongue dipped inside me. "Matisse?"

"Hmm?" I murmured.

He carefully shifted my feet so my legs were spread, giving him more access. "I'm going to make you come so hard you're not going to be able to hold yourself up."

"Oh, okay," I whispered and buried my hands in his thick hair, my hips swaying with anticipation.

"Then I'm going to carry you to the bed, bury myself deep inside you, and claim you in the way only a man who's had every part of you can."

"Uh-huh," I agreed, trembling now. "Yes. Do it now. Make me come for you." In my lust-filled state, I didn't care that I was begging. Didn't care that I was at his mercy. He wanted to make me feel things I'd never let myself feel before, that loss of control while being pleasured by another. I wanted it. Craved it. And trusted him to be the one to do it.

His tongue darted out, licking my hot, slick flesh with practiced expertise. The orgasm started to build instantly. My magic sprang to life with each stroke of his tongue, as if his touch was calling my power forward. I had no control over it. Couldn't stop it even if I wanted to. Not that I did. The sensation was heady and bringing me to the edge faster than ever before.

I moaned, magic sparking around me.

Vaughn raised his head, meeting my half-lidded eyes. His were full of untamed lust, and without warning, his fingers plunged into me as he sucked hard on my sensitive flesh.

My entire body trembled as a long, slow shudder rolled through me.

Sparks of magic flickered over my skin, serving only to intensify the glorious sensations. I'd never felt this good before. Never felt this alive. I rocked my hips forward, demanding more.

That clever mouth of his sucked harder. My muscles tightened, and a ragged gasp escaped me as the bundle of nerves went off like a rocket. The orgasm hit me fast and hard. If Vaughn hadn't been holding me up, I was certain I'd slide to the floor of the shower. But his strong hands kept me in place. And all the while he kept his tongue on me, coaxing me into a greater frenzy of sensation.

I bit my lower lip, trying to hold back the screams of release, but I lost the battle and cried out his name, confirming that at least for that night, I did belong to him.

He held me there under the warm stream of water, his head pressed to my stomach as he waited for my shudders to fade away.

I wasn't sure what to say. He'd made another promise. The one to claim me, to really mark me as his. Would he do it?

I didn't have to wait long for my answer. Without a word, Vaughn flipped the water off and secured me in his arms. A moment later, he was on top of me in his bed, reaching for a condom. "Remember what I said before?"

I nodded.

"Good. Because I want you more than I've ever wanted anyone."

As he deftly rolled the condom on, I jerked up and caught his lower lip in mine, sucking on his the way he'd been sucking on me less than a few minutes before. He groaned, and true to his word, he slammed into me, burying himself deep.

"Ohh," I sighed, wrapping myself around him. "Yes."

Our eyes met. In him, I saw a man I could finally trust to take me places I'd been too afraid to go before. Magic crackled around us, forming a cocoon of light.

Vaughn froze, taking in the fireworks show, but when I lifted my hips, creating that sweet friction, his attention snapped back to me. Then he started to move. He pulled back slowly, savoring the incredible torture. I clutched at his arms, digging my nails in, silently begging him to give me what I so obviously craved. He paused, staring down at me, his expression focused.

"Please," I said.

That one word unraveled his control and he thrust into me. Magic rippled over my skin and then clung to him. I knew the moment he felt it. His hips jerked and he slid into me—deeper, if that was even possible.

"Shit, Matisse. You feel so damn good."

I could only manage a nod. His touch was now sending tingles of delight into me at every spot we connected. It was overwhelming and intoxicating at the same time. The magic was wholly intertwined with our lovemaking now. With each stroke, each movement we made together, the magic got stronger. It encircled us and built to dizzying levels.

He gazed down at me in wonder. Our eyes locked, and together we moved in unison. We were lost in the moment, magic coursing through the both of us, spilling all around us, and building with each moment we were lost in each other.

The fire building inside me raged hotter and wilder than ever before. I matched his pace, raising my hips to meet his as he made me his in mind, body, and soul.

I was lost in the haze of sex and magic.

"Are you with me, Mati?" Vaughn's husky voice brought me back to myself.

Nodding, I tightened my grip on his shoulders.

"Good, baby. That's good. Do you like the way I feel inside of you?"

"Yes." My voice was barely a whisper.

"How much?"

"Hmm. A lot," I muttered into his shoulder as I clung to him, trying to get closer.

"Show me."

His words were like a drug possessing me. I hooked one leg around his and we rolled together until I was straddling him.

"Ride me," Vaughn commanded.

And even though I was on top, he was still in charge. His hands clasped my hips as he held me in place and thrust up into me. I moaned as the crescendo of pleasure flooded my senses. Another thrust. And another, as magic filled the room, bursting around us. I gasped as Vaughn ground into me one last time and we came together. The second orgasm bolted through me, hitting me so hard I collapsed against him, gasping for breath.

He kissed my shoulder and brought his hand up to gently caress my face. We stared at each other, each of us wide-eyed. He had a look of wonder, but all I felt was empty, and it scared the crap out of me.

"Vaughn," I said and tried to lift myself off him, but I was too weak. Instead, I sort of slid to the side, one leg still draped over his body.

"Mati?" His voice was far away and my vision started to fade. Then there was nothing.

Chapter 12

Vaughn

Confusion mixed with panic lined Matisse's face as she collapsed at my side.

I sprang up and clasped her shoulders. "Matisse? Babe. What's wrong?"

Nothing. She didn't move and her body appeared to be totally limp. "Shit!" I climbed to my knees and scooped her up in my arms, holding her close. She'd spent too much of her magic. I was sure of it. Never in my life had I felt someone throw that much power around. I'd thought it had all been part of her sex-witch ritual, but now, seeing her unconscious, my gut told me something had gone terribly wrong.

"Wake up," I said gently and brushed her hair back, panic slowly taking over. "Matisse, wake up!" I shook her gently. Her head lolled to one side. "Dammit!"

I positioned her head on a pillow and leaped off the bed. Pulling on fresh jeans, I grabbed my phone. Except I wasn't sure who to call. A doctor? Her mom? Mitch? No, not him. Her coven. They'd know what to do. I ran into the other room and grabbed my notebook, which was full of supernatural contacts. After flipping to the correct page, I dialed.

"Coven Pointe Charms," a woman said.

"I'm looking for your coven leader. It's an emergency."

"Who is this?"

"Vaughn Paxton. One of your members is here. Matisse, and she's ill. It's imperative that I speak with your leader."

"Matisse?"

"Yes, dammit."

"What happened? Can you put her—"

Crash!

A clamoring came from my living room. I spun and ran, hearing nothing but the sound of my heart in my throat. Had another demon come after Matisse?

But when I slid to a stop in my doorway, there wasn't a demon. There was a man untangling himself from an extension cord that connected my television to an outlet on an adjoining wall.

"What the hell are you doing in my house?" I demanded.

The tall man with brilliant green eyes smiled and held his hand out.

I ignored it. "I said—"

A fog settled over my brain. My thoughts jumbled as if my brain had been scrambled. Then my arm rose on its own and I shook the man's hand.

He gave me a warm smile. "Welcome to the Brotherhood, Vaughn. We were hoping you'd join us soon."

I heard the words but couldn't process them. All I could do was nod.

"If you're ready, I'd be pleased to take you to headquarters."

There was a nagging somewhere in the back of my mind. I was forgetting something important. But it wouldn't come. "Yes," I heard myself say.

"Excellent." The man, dressed in a black jacket and jeans, positioned himself next to me, grabbed my hand, and then took a step forward.

The world turned gray as air rushed over my skin. I blinked, and my surroundings morphed again. We stood on a sidewalk in front of a large white antebellum home with a white picket fence.

"Welcome home," my escort said.

I glanced from him to the house. The yard was lush and green with an old majestic oak taking up residence on the left side of the lawn. I had a sense of belonging, and I never wanted to leave. Without hesitation, I followed my escort up the walk and into the large house.

Seven figures all dressed the same were lined up in the large foyer. The one in the middle, the oldest, lifted his gaze and said in a formal tone, "Vaughn Paxton, welcome to the Brotherhood."

I didn't know what the Brotherhood was, but there was a feeling deep in my gut that this was where I was supposed to be. It felt right. Like something important was happening. Without being told, I was sure that man was the leader. I nodded, waiting for instruction.

The leader turned and walked through double doors. The other brothers surrounded me, and as a unit, we all followed him into a grand ballroom. The leader stood waiting for us in the middle of the room. The other seven men fanned out, forming a half circle around him.

"Vaughn, please take your place in the middle of the circle."

Stuck in a trancelike state, I did as I was told. The moment my feet stilled, the confusion lifted and my memories came rushing back in. Matisse. She needed my help.

Rage filled me. I'd been spelled or possessed or something. Otherwise, I would've never left Matisse. Who were these people? Why was I here? I didn't even want to find out. With single-minded determination, I spun and took off toward the exit. Only when I got to the edge of the circle, I slammed into an invisible wall and bounced back.

"What the fuck is—"

More memories flooded my brain. Only they weren't mine. They were like a movie reel of past events. Demons were everywhere. And angels. And witches like Matisse. Battles were being fought. Angels fell. Others were kidnapped and forced into Hell until they fell. It was an all-out war full of chaos. Demons ruled and did unspeakable acts to witches and humans.

The despair and heartache rushed through me, seized me, gutted me. Created an intense need to do something. Anything to help the poor souls who were being destroyed.

Then the reel changed, and another group of witches appeared. They were locked up in some facet of Hell, waiting. Most of them were resigned. A few were angry, and still others were just plain broken. A fierce desire to help them overtook me, but there was nothing I could do about a memory.

The fact that they were trapped was bad enough, but then a group of lesser demons descended on them, and the reason for their entrapment was clear. They were sex slaves. Utter disgust rolled through me. Why was I being shown this? Was this happening right now? The need to protect, to fight for justice, seized me.

"Vaughn Paxton, do you willingly submit to spending the rest of your days as a demon hunter? To devote your life to fighting demons and protecting those who cannot protect themselves?"

My consent was on the tip of my tongue, almost as if it was being forced from me. Yes. I would do that. Nothing could stop me. But then Matisse's image flashed in my mind. What had happened to her? And why had these people come for me now? Did it have to do with her?

A new reel of what had to be history flickered to life in my mind. The scene of the lesser demons and witches reappeared, only it must have been a different day. The witches appeared to be a few years younger than they had been. The light faded and the demons and witches faded with it, save but two. One demon and one witch.

Only instead of being afraid, the witch appeared to like the lesser demon. And he appeared to be in love with her. With these two, there was no forced sex. They were deeply in love. And after they joined for the first time, the witch gave every last bit of her magic and power to the demon, leaving herself on the verge of death.

But the demon, he morphed from a demon to something else. Something more than he was before. Moral. Determined. Honorable. Power radiated from him. He sank to his knees, gathered his witch in his arms, and bolted, determined to use his newfound power to protect her from the life she'd been forced into.

The leader studied me. "That memory is how the first incubus came into being."

"Incubus?" I said, my tone low. Unease settled over me. "Why are you telling me this?"

"Your witch unleashed your power, Vaughn. You were born an incubus. And by birthright, destined to be part of the Brotherhood, an organization fully dedicated to fighting the existence of demons." He waved a hand around the room. "Welcome home."

An incubus. How could that be true? But a voice deep down whispered, *How could it not be?* The years of having any woman I wanted. The undeniable sex appeal. The way Matisse had called to me.

Matisse. Holy fuck. Her image once again haunted me. I had to see her. I'd been the one who'd broken her. I had to make sure she was all right.

"Do you, Vaughn, accept the induction into the Brotherhood?" the leader asked once more.

I crossed my arms over my chest, and with a will greater than I knew I possessed, I said, "No. I do not accept. Now let me the hell out of here."

The circle tightened around me and the images became more vivid, more horrid, assaulting me to the point I wanted to gag. With a roar, I sprang forward and grabbed the leader by his shirt, pulling him up close. "What the hell are you doing, old man?"

He stood still, unaffected by my assault.

"Speak up!" I shook him, trying to elicit a response. Any at all.

"Release me, Vaughn." His tone was mild, unconcerned.

Despite my anger, something unexplainable came over me and I stepped back, but that didn't stop me from giving the bastard a push.

He swayed, took one unsure step, and then righted himself. "Are you prepared to reject your birthright, to let the innocent suffer, to let the demons corrupt our world? To corrupt you? Your power will be too much to handle without the Brotherhood. Eventually you'll fall—become a full-blown demon."

I glared at him. They'd taken me from Matisse when she needed me most. How was that protecting people? "Cut the shit. I'm not buying your Brotherhood bullshit or your demon scare tactics. What is it you want from me exactly?" Humans couldn't fall. Only angels could. That much I knew. But I wasn't human, was I? No. He'd said incubus. Anger coiled in my gut. Everything about this was too forced. Too heavy-handed.

He met my eyes, then nodded to one of the brothers. Without a word, the seven of them filed out of the great hall.

The leader held his hand out. "I'm Maximus. It's a pleasure to finally meet you."

I ignored his hand and waited.

"Come with me." Maximus crossed the room and opened a door into what appeared to be his private office.

I glanced back at the foyer. I couldn't waste any more time here. Matisse was sick.

"She's being taken care of," Maximus said.

"Excuse me?"

"Your witch. She's being taken care of. Soon after you were transported here, her people came for her. Even if you went back to your place, you wouldn't find her."

"How do you know that?" I was about half a second from tearing out of there to find out for myself.

He waved a hand, and a projection lit the ballroom wall. It was a scene in my apartment. The demon hunter and I vanished into thin air, and a moment later, a woman who had to be Matisse's mom burst through my front door. Another woman followed, and the pair searched my apartment until they found

Matisse unconscious on my bed. I watched the silent film as the pair stuffed a variety of herbals down her throat and cast some spell.

Matisse's eyes fluttered open briefly, and she mouthed something that looked like "Vaughn."

Relief at seeing her awake did nothing to squelch my desire to find her at any cost. I still needed to see for myself that she was going to be okay.

But the scene morphed and then Matisse was walking up the stairs to a shotgun double style house. Although she was clearly worn out, she was moving under her own steam. The knot in my chest eased, and I was finally able to breathe. "She's with her family, then?"

Maximus nodded. "She'll be fine."

"What happened to her?"

He cast me a sympathetic glance that only served to piss me off. "Come into my office and I'll explain."

Reluctantly, I followed the man because if nothing else, I was going to get answers.

Chapter 13

Matisse

The last thing I remembered was being joined with Vaughn, magic pulsing around us in a heady stream of power. It had been intense, freeing, and I'd been completely in the moment, giving myself over to him. I'd loved it. And when we'd come together, something had exploded inside me and set my magic free.

But then as the elation of incredible sex had started to fade away, my head started swimming and my limbs became weak. I'd reached for Vaughn, but my strength was gone.

Everything had gone black.

I don't know how long I faded in and out of consciousness, but when I did finally wake, I was still in Vaughn's bed and my mother was hovering over me.

"Mati?" Her light blue eyes were narrowed and shining with concern.

"Mom?" My voice sounded far away. "What's going on? Where's Vaughn?"

She ran a soothing hand over my brow. "He had to go, love. Don't worry about him right now."

"Tell the girl the truth, Maven," Dayla, my aunt, said harshly. "She has a right to know."

I rubbed my eyes and tried to focus on Dayla, but she was only a blur. "Tell me what?"

"Never mind that now." My mom's tone was full of irritation. "There's plenty of time to fill her in later. It's not like he's coming back."

That made me sit up. The world spun as the sheet fell, leaving me exposed to my mother and aunt. I clutched at the sheet and huddled back down in the bed. "Can someone get me my clothes?"

"They're right here," Mom said. "Let's get you dressed and take you home."

I was too weak to argue and let my mom help me get dressed for the first time since I was six years old. Before long, they had me tucked in Mom's Range Rover and then we were flying through the streets of New Orleans on the way back to the Pointe. I stared out the window, clutching my chest. The emptiness claiming my insides was almost too much to bear. Tears burned the backs of my eyes. And I did nothing to stop them from streaming down my face.

When we pulled up in front of Mom's house, Dayla took one look at me and swore. "Look at what he's done to her. Tell her everything right now, or I will." She turned to me. "Matisse, pull yourself together. You need to be strong now."

Mom sent her a dirty look. "Give her five minutes. Jeez." Mom took me by the hand and led me to her guest room. "Lie down and I'll bring you some healing tea."

I climbed on the bed and curled up into a ball. There was no fight in me. There was nothing.

Sometime later, Mom came back, holding a tray with tea and some soup. "How are you, baby?"

I peered up at her. Mom wasn't the coddling type. I didn't think I'd ever heard her call me baby. Not even when I was a little girl. "What is it?"

She set the tray down and blew out a breath. "How long have you known Vaughn?"

"Just a few days. Why?"

She shook her head, her expression skeptical. "That's all?"

"Yes."

"It's even worse than I thought." She stood and paced the room, her bare feet silent on the wood floors.

I rolled over to my back and stared up at her.

"You're not going to like this," she said.

"Well, with a buildup like that…"

She chuckled, then sobered as she sat next to me. "Vaughn is an incubus."

"Umm… what?" Did she just say what I thought she did? I tried to scramble so I was sitting up, but my arms were too weak and my head too heavy. Giving up, I flopped back down on the bed and hugged a pillow. "I had sex with a demon?" I whispered, utterly horrified.

"Oh, no." She wrapped her warm hand around my cold one. "He's a descendant of a demon, which makes him predisposed to be an incubus, but the only way to awaken that side of him is to have sex with a sex witch."

I frowned, confused. "Having sex with me turned him into an incubus?"

"Yes. But it's not just the sex. He must have gained your trust somehow."

Well, he had. I'd opened up to him and shed my guards. "What does that have to do with anything?"

"Everything. You had to have given him some of your magic in order to ignite the shift from human to incubus."

Dread filled all the empty crevices in my chest. I *had* done that. I'd thought I'd been letting the magic build for myself. That afterward, I'd have plenty of reserves. And instead, he'd stolen it. And then left me for dead.

The bastard!

When I saw him next, I'd kill him. Rip his heart out and feed it to the gators. No wonder he'd been so hell-bent on saving me from the demon. He needed me for his own devious plans. I'd opened myself up for the first time, and he'd taken advantage of me in the worst way possible. He'd stolen the most important part of me. My magic.

"How do you know this?" I asked her, my voice getting weaker by the moment.

Dayla, whom I hadn't even known was in the room, came into view. She placed her palm on my cheek and stared into my eyes. "Because, darling. It happened to me once. Incubi need sex witches to complete the change. And they'll do whatever they have to in order to make it happen. Including breaking your heart."

She knew. She understood what I'd given up without my knowledge.

"Sleep, my lovely niece. We'll talk more when you get your strength back."

I wanted to ask more questions. Wanted to know everything about what had happened and how long it would take to recover, but I couldn't. My eyes closed and the world faded away.

———

I spent three and a half weeks on bed rest. The night I'd spent with Vaughn had taken more than my magic. He'd taken away my ability to live any sort of normal life. I slept twenty hours a day for the first week. I couldn't concentrate on my schoolwork and ended up taking an incomplete in all my classes. I'd have to retake them all.

Plus my power was all but gone. Replenishing it would require sleeping with someone else. That was the last thing I wanted to do. It was almost as if I had PTSD. Even after I built up a little strength, I had no interest in trolling for a sex partner.

The day after I moved back into my apartment, I was sitting on my couch shoveling ice cream in my face when a knock sounded on the door. I didn't even look up. Whoever it was could just go away.

But no matter how much I ignored the knocking, the person wouldn't stop. Finally I got up, wrapped a blanket around my shoulders, and flung the door open. "What?"

Chessa stood on my porch, one eyebrow raised in curiosity. "Is this what your life is going to be now?"

I stared at her open-mouthed. Then, without a word, I spun and headed back to my couch.

She closed the door and followed me. "You can't go on acting as if you're not a witch."

The coffee-flavored ice cream melted over my tongue. Swallowing, I made a point of shoveling another large spoonful into my mouth.

She shook her head and sat in the chair across from me. "Are you going to let him ruin your life?"

I knew what she was doing. She wanted to get me so pissed that I got my fire back. What she didn't understand was that my fire was gone. Stolen. I couldn't help her. "There's nothing left, Chessa."

"There is. You just have to see your way through it."

"Riiight. I'll get right on that." I dug into the ice cream, scooping up another large portion. "The only way I'm going to get my magic back is by sleeping with someone. And that's not going to happen. Never again. Got it? I was used. Violated. And I'll never put myself in that position again. So go back to the realm and find someone else to help you with the portal, because I'm out."

She stood and placed her hands on her hips. "You weren't violated. Not in the way you think."

I jumped to my feet and got in her face. "You have no idea what you're talking about, *angel.*"

Chessa blew out a breath, clearly trying to stay calm. "You can be as mad at me as you want to. I can take it. But I'm here to tell you the whole truth, not Dayla's distorted view. I'm an angel. We devote our lives to fighting demons. That means I have a little better idea of what goes down, don't you think?"

I shrugged. Maybe, but what did that have to do with Vaughn?

"Incubi are rare. When they are made—"

"You mean after they steal the magic of a sex witch?" I said dryly.

"Well, that's one way to look at it. But not all of them know that's what they're doing. You can't know if Vaughn was using you or if you just happened to connect. A man who is predisposed to become an incubus has a sexual energy that's hard to ignore. Just like a sex witch. Though sex witches know this about themselves and use it to their advantage."

"Hey!" I tossed my spoon down. "I was out gathering magic for your project. Don't judge me."

"I'm not." She stepped back, clearly offended I would think such a thing of her.

Whatever. She had no idea what it was like to be me right then.

"I'm saying he might not have known. All of this might have been as big of a shock to him as it was to you. That's all." She backed up and clasped her hand over the doorknob. "Think about it, Mati. Who targeted whom?"

Startled, I jerked my head up and met her eyes. I had targeted him. He'd approached me only after I'd made my presence known. But... "If he didn't know and this was all a massive mistake, then where has he been? He's a tracker. If he wanted to find me, he could've."

She shook her head. "I don't know. But wouldn't it be better if you knew the truth?"

I averted my gaze. Did I want the truth? What if everything I feared was true? What if it wasn't? Either way, was I going to sit on my couch for the rest of my life wallowing in my Blue Bell ice cream? Seeing Chessa standing there and treating me as if I weren't broken lit a fire in my belly. Was I going to let him ruin my life? Eff that. I glanced back up and met her penetrating gaze. "I have someone I can call. I'll have my magic back in a few days. Come back then. I'll be ready to work."

"That's not—"

"It's all you're getting." I didn't want to sleep with anyone, but if I was honest with myself, I missed my magic. Was lost without it.

She let out a long breath. "I was going to say I didn't come here to put you back to work. I came to make sure you're okay. But do what you have to do."

I plucked at the blanket. "Chess?"

"Yeah?"

"I have nothing. No school. No job without my magic. And even Ashley's avoiding me right now. I don't blame her. I've not been myself."

She eyed the ice cream and snorted. "Some things haven't changed."

That made me smile. "Right, well… Anyway. I need something for me. And as long as I can get my magic back, I want to keep working with you."

"Good." She pulled the door open. "Call me when you're ready."

Chapter 14

Vaughn

I was in my new house unpacking my extensive book collection when the doorbell rang. I frowned. No one knew where I lived. And there was a spell on the house to keep strangers away. Who could possibly be on the other side of that door?

Maximus was my guess. That guy just wouldn't leave well enough alone. No matter how many times I refused to join the demon hunters, he kept coming back. Why couldn't he understand that I couldn't commit my life to something that was only available to me by stealing magic from someone I cared about? The idea I was susceptible to becoming a demon bothered me, but I wasn't willing to be ruled by fear.

I'd been by Matisse's apartment a few times, but her friend had said she was with her mom for the time being. I hadn't had the balls to go looking for her there. Call me a coward, but a house full of witches was more than a little intimidating. Besides, what I had to say to Matisse was private.

I crossed through the living room to the small entry of my Lakeview home and peered through the peephole. I recognized her immediately, with her dark hair and intense, dark eyes. Matisse's mother. What was she doing here? And how had she found my new place? I pulled the door open and leaned against the frame. "Good evening, Ms. Ballintine. It's a pleasure to see you."

She frowned, clearly unhappy to be there. "Can I come in?"

I stepped aside, gesturing her into the entry hall.

She walked in straight to my empty living room. "No furniture?"

"It hasn't been delivered yet." I nodded toward the kitchen. "I do have stools, though."

"Fine."

I led the way and waited for her to sit. Her hostility should have put me off, but I found it more interesting than anything. It had been weeks since my night with Matisse. Why was her mother here now? Unless Ashley had been mistaken and Mati wasn't getting stronger with each day. "How is Matisse? Is she okay?"

"She's fine. Or will be. And that's why I'm here."

I hated myself for hurting her. It didn't matter that it had been unintentional. I was gutted by the knowledge. "What can I do?"

"Nothing." Her eyes narrowed as she studied me. "That's what I came to say. I know you've gone by her place at least once. Do me a favor and stay away. Nothing good can come of a visit from you. You'll only make matters worse."

"I need to apologize," I said. "I don't want to do anything to harm her. Quite the opposite, and she deserves to hear what I have to say."

"Maybe she does. In that case, put it in a letter." She stood. "Because if you go see her now, I'm fairly certain she'll have a mental breakdown. But not before she tries to spell your dick off." Her tone was matter-of-fact, as if she hadn't just mentioned Matisse castrating me. "Got it?"

I nodded, not at all sure what I was supposed to say to that. But if Matisse really was that angry with me, if I did show up now, it would only serve to delay her healing. I could and would wait it out. "For now."

"What does that mean, for now? Haven't you done enough damage?"

"No doubt. But that doesn't mean I'm not going to find a way to make it right someday." Matisse's mother could think anything she wanted. It wouldn't change the fact that even after only two days together, I cared about her daughter. Cared more than I should.

She scowled. "There's no way to make it right." Then she closed her eyes and took a deep breath. "Never mind. Just stay away from her. If not, you'll have me to answer to."

"Understood."

Matisse

It took me all day to make the damned phone call. It shouldn't have been that hard. Sex wasn't a big deal. At least it hadn't been. Now? I felt differently. What I'd shared with Vaughn had changed me. Now sex held meaning. Just the thought of being with someone else made my stomach hurt.

But at the same time, if I was able to help Chessa close the portal and cut off the demons, she'd be safer. And just maybe that would mean there would be less need for incubi. Maybe it was stupid, but if I could save one sex witch from feeling as used and violated as I had, it would be worth it.

The fact that I was going to use Brandon was not lost on me. The best I could do was to be up front with him from the beginning. Make sure he knew this was only about the physical act in order to get strong again. As a witch, he'd understand what I meant.

The phone rang only once before he picked up. "Mati! What's up?"

"Hey, you. Are you busy?" I held my breath. He could have a date... or even a girlfriend by now. It had been four weeks since I'd seen him.

"Not right now. Just sitting here thinking about going out for a beer. Why?"

I sucked in a nervous breath. The feeling was so unnatural. I was never nervous around the opposite sex. It was part of my gift. "I was wondering if you might want to come over for a while. I, ah… Damn. Look, I need to get strong and I'm not up for spending time with a random stranger."

Silence.

"Brandon?"

He cleared his throat. "I'm here."

"Did you hear what I said?"

He chuckled. "I heard you. Just took me a moment to process. I've never been propositioned like that before."

"Oh, crap." I sat on my couch and hung my head, keeping the phone pressed to my ear. "I'm sorry. Forget I even called. It was a stupid idea."

"No!" Another pause. "I mean no, it wasn't stupid. And it's fine. We're friends. Of course I can help you out. But are you sure you want me to come to your place? That's unusual for you, isn't it?"

Instead of relief, a strange trace of trepidation shuddered through me. But I shut my feelings down. This wasn't about me and my desires. It was about getting healthy enough to go back to work. "I'm sure." If anything went wrong, I didn't want to end up naked and passed out in someone else's space. Never again.

"Okay. What time?"

"Now?" Goddess. That sounded desperate. I bit my lip and waited for him to laugh.

But he didn't. "Sure." His voice had turned husky. "See you soon."

Vaughn

After Matisse's mother left, Mitch called. He had another job for me. I changed into dark jeans, a gray hoodie, and black boots. To someone who didn't know me, I could be a student or I could be a drug dealer. Both were good cover options considering I was heading to Mitch's neighborhood.

His house was in Mid-City, not too far from City Park. It wasn't the best neighborhood, but it wasn't the worst either. The paint on his shotgun double was peeling and the porch sagged with years of neglect. It's not a place I would've chosen to live, but if the rent was low enough, I guess the house and large yard afforded him some privacy.

I knocked once and then let myself in. The front room was virtually empty, not a stick of furniture in the place. "Mitch?"

"In the kitchen." His voice floated from the back of the house.

I found him at a Formica table. His laptop was open and files covered every inch of the surface. "Good. You're here." He stood up and passed me a beer.

I took it but made no move to actually drink it. "You have a job for me?"

"Yes." He rifled through the papers on the table, his movements jerky and overly excited. Looking up, he called, "Sam! He's here."

Light footsteps sounded on the hardwood floors. My eyes widened and then narrowed when my old friend came into view. She seemed even smaller than her five-foot three frame. Her hair was rumpled and her face was blotchy from crying.

"Sam?" I met my best friend from high school in the kitchen doorway and caught her as she flung herself into my waiting arms. "What happened?"

"Where were you?" she said, her words muffled against my shoulder.

I caressed her hair, trying to soothe her as she shook in my arms. "When? Today? I was at home."

She pulled back, her pale blue eyes fiery with anger. "No. A month ago when I came to your shop. You said you'd always be there for me. But the one time I needed you, you weren't. And no one there would give me your number or address."

A faint recollection of Rick telling me a woman had come by to see me resurfaced from my memory. "I'm so sorry. They didn't tell me who it was. Otherwise I…" I clutched her shoulders and took a good look at the faint bruises on her neck and temple. My muscles tightened with all-consuming anger. "Who did this to you?"

Her lip trembled, but she sucked in a breath and forced out, "My ex."

"That son of a bitch." Wilson Waters. I'd never liked him and now I knew why. "I'll kill him."

I was halfway across the kitchen, determined to go after Wilson, when Mitch said, "He's a witch."

"So," I said and kept walking.

"He's dabbling with black magic." Mitch's tone was laced with excitement, making me pause. "After you find him, bring him to me."

I turned and met his impassive eyes. Maybe I'd imagined the excitement. "Why? If he's using black magic isn't it better to call the Witches' Council for an immediate pickup?"

"Not this time. Sam says he's working on black curses designed to be used on other people. If that's the case, we need to find out if he has any cohorts. The Council won't share their findings with us. If we want to keep New Orleans safe, that's information we need to know."

Keep New Orleans safe? I'd never known Mitch to give two shits about anyone but himself. Maybe seeing Sam battered had awoken his conscience. One could hope. "If you say so."

Sam hurried across the room and grabbed my arm. "I'm going with you."

"I don't think that's a good idea," I said, gently removing her arm from mine.

"Too damn bad." She scowled at me. "I'm the one he's been beating the last month, and I'm the one who knows exactly where he'll be. I want to be there when you take his ass down. After the last police report, he promised to put me six feet under. I intend to see with my own two eyes that he gets exactly what he deserves."

Fuck me. He'd been beating her for over a month. He'd threatened her life. And I'd moved and changed my number so often she hadn't been able to easily get in touch with me. I tugged her to my side, wanting to hold on to her forever. She was the sister I never had. "How did you find Mitch?"

"A friend of a friend knew how to get in touch with a witch connected with the Council. I didn't know it was Mitch until he opened his front door." She glanced at the clock on the wall. "I know where he'll be for the next hour. We should go."

Goddammit. My self-loathing intensified. She was here by pure chance. No doubt she'd suffered more than she would even let on. I wanted to tuck her into my house and leave her there until I was certain this bastard was incarcerated, but I knew her better than that. She'd never go for it. "You're staying in the car."

Her posture didn't relax, but I did sense a small bit of relief in her expression. "Fine."

"Remember. Bring him here before calling the Council," Mitch said.

"Sure." I held my hand out to Sam. "Ready?"

"More than ever."

Once outside, I opened the passenger door of the SUV for Sam and then climbed into the driver's side. "Want to talk about it?" I asked.

"No. I have a therapist." Her tone was firm. End of discussion.

"Got it." I pulled away from the curb, heading in the direction of the university. "And you're here now because things have escalated?"

She scoffed. "Escalated. Right. Yeah, when the death threats started, I figured it was time to take matters into my own hands."

"Shit, Sam. I'm sorry." I was fucking up all over the place with the women in my life.

"You should be. I needed you." She crossed her arms over her chest and dug her fingernails into her forearms.

"You won't have any issues getting in touch with me for now on," I vowed. "Tell me about the black magic. I need to know what I'm up against."

She went pale as the blood drained from her face. "He's researching a Black Heart spell. It's cast on witches and affects the people they fall in love with. It usually ends in death."

Horror rushed into me. "And he wanted to use this on...?"

"My new boyfriend. He's a witch, but I don't want him involved in this. He'll try to kill Wilson."

"Shit!"

"That's what I'm sayin'. Now hurry up. He's hosting a weekly meeting for one of his frat committees."

"He's a frat guy?" Damn. I supposed everyone loved him, too. Classic abuser situation.

She didn't respond and only spoke again to give me directions. We parked in front of a two-story craftsman house and waited until half a dozen college guys filed out of the front door.

"Which level does he live on?" I asked.

"Bottom. Apartment 1A."

"Got it. Sit tight." I grabbed my stun gun and zip ties. I could've used a tranq dart, but that would've been too kind for the likes of this bastard.

I didn't bother trying to be stealth bounty hunter guy. Waters was going to know exactly why I'd come for him. The door was open a few inches, and instead of knocking, I strode right in. "Waters?" I called.

The tall blond guy appeared from what must have been a bedroom. When he met my eyes, he scowled. "Paxton, what the fuck do you want?"

"To kick your ass." I took two steps and slammed my fist into his nose. He howled and crumpled at my feet. Idiot. He hadn't even seen it coming.

Magic gathered around him, but before he could cast any spell, I slammed my boot into his gut. The power dissipated. He wasn't a very strong witch, was he? Normally when witches were pissed their power raged out of control. His reaction implied he was scared.

Recoiling, he rolled and grunted. Staring up at me with hatred in his eyes, he asked, "What the fuck is your problem?"

I leaned down so our faces were inches apart. "My problem, jackass, is that you seem to think it's fun to beat on women. This is the last time you raise a fist to anyone." I was dying to break another rib or two, but the bastard wasn't fighting back. Instead, I put my foot on his back and held him down as I reached for my zip ties.

The door slammed open and Sam stood in the threshold, shaking with anger. Before I could stop her, she was by my side, slamming her foot into his side, yelling at the top of her lungs. "You son of a bitch! Think you can threaten me? Think you can force me to sleep with you? I told you, you'd regret the day you ever met me!"

"Sam!" I grabbed her arms and pulled her back. "That's enough."

She turned on me, daggers shooting from her blue eyes. "It will never be enough." A sob got caught in her throat as she collapsed against me.

A groan came from Waters, and then I felt his magic build again. It was stronger and more forceful than before. I spun, shielding Sam from him. My stun gun was in my hand, but before I could connect with him, a blast of magic came from across the room. The light slammed into Waters and he went limp, his face white.

"That should keep him under control." A petite older witch stood just inside the door. Her hair was pulled back into a severe bun.

Sam stepped out from behind me. "Ms. Anders?"

I glanced between the two of them. "What's going on?"

The older witch strode forward and held her hand out to me. "I'm a professor at the University. I also happen to work for the Witches' Council. We got a tip about Waters early this morning. I've been watching him ever since." She turned to

Sam. "I assume you won't have any problems testifying against the accused?"

She shook her head. "None at all. He sent me a threatening message late this morning. Again. I thought I was his only target." She swallowed. "Did he, um, hurt someone else?"

Ms. Anders' expression turned to one of pity. "He tried. But she escaped."

"That's good," Sam said in a small voice.

The older witch turned to me. "Thank you for your help, Mr. Paxton. The Council will take it from here."

I wasn't surprised she knew who I was. Bounty hunters were fully vetted before we were approved to freelance. Mitch was going to be upset he wasn't going to be able to interrogate Waters, but there was nothing I could do about it now. I inclined my head. "Glad to be of service."

Sam clutched my hand and squeezed.

I pulled her into a hug and whispered, "Are you going to be okay? Do you want me to stay with you?"

She shook her head. "I'm fine now."

"You're positive?"

Nodding, she stepped out of my embrace. "I'll call you later. Don't change your number again."

I gave her a small smile. "If I do, you'll be the first to know. Don't forget to tell the Council about the black magic."

"I won't." She kissed my cheek. "Thanks for the help."

"Anytime, Sam. You know that." I nodded to the Council witch and took off, ready to give Mitch the bad news.

Chapter 15

Matisse

I sat on my couch, tapping my foot. Brandon was supposed to arrive in less than ten minutes. My nerves were about to choke me. I knew this was something I had to do, but my insides weren't really on board.

The doorbell rang, and I nearly jumped right off the sofa. Damn, Mati. Get your shit together. It's just Brandon.

When I opened the door, he leaned down and gave me a kiss on my cheek. It was a sweet gesture. One that he'd made dozens of times before. Then why was I recoiling?

"Hey. You doing okay?" he asked, concern radiating from his eyes.

"Yeah. You?"

He linked his arm around my shoulders and led me back to my couch. "Great."

We sat and even though he was relaxed and made no mention of the fact I'd essentially invited him over for a booty call, I felt so incredibly awkward I didn't know what to do. Television maybe? I reached for the remote, but in my haste, I bumped my glass and water splattered all over the coffee table.

"Oh, damn!" I jumped up and ran for the hallway linen closet. When I got back, Brandon was clearing magazines and rescuing my remote from the river of water. "Thank you," I said as I wiped up the mess.

"No problem."

It took me a moment to realize he was standing there studying me. I straightened. "What?"

"You seem… different."

"Different?" I folded my hands together and took a step back. "Different how?"

He shook his head. "Just different. Less cocky I guess."

That was probably a fair assessment. Ever since my last night with Vaughn, my confidence had fled. And I wasn't interested in flirting with or tormenting anyone of the opposite sex. It's why I'd called him. I couldn't stomach any of those things. I shrugged. "I'm just depleted I guess."

He gazed down at me and then smiled, holding out his hand. I didn't move.

"Mati?" he asked gently.

"What?"

"It's okay. We're friends, remember?"

He seemed so relaxed, so unconcerned about anything, that it made me want to curl into him and forget everything. I moved toward him and instead of taking his hand, I wrapped my arms around him, pressing my cheek to his shoulder. His capable arms encircled me as he stroked my hair. It was nice, but not at all sexy in any way. How was I going to get through this?

Good God. I was a sex witch. How was I ever going to cast another spell if I couldn't find the courage to get on with it?

Brandon took the wet towel from me and hung it in my bathroom. When he got back, he tugged me down onto the couch, tucking me into the crook of his arm. "Just relax."

"I can't."

He chuckled. "I can see that. But seriously, Mati, we don't have to do anything. I came over because you asked me to, not because I want to get laid."

I pulled back and gave him a dubious look. "Really?"

His chuckle turned into a full-blown laugh. "Well, I wouldn't mind getting laid. Especially if the activity involves you, but that's not the primary reason I'm here. I'd have shown up even if you'd said you were going to force me to watch *Real Housewives* all night."

"Seriously? *Real Housewives?* You've lost your damned mind. I would never ask you or anyone else to watch that all night. Talk about drama overload."

"See?" He brushed a lock of hair out of my eyes. "That's how much I care."

"More than I deserve." I smiled up at him. Then I leaned in and brushed my lips over his. In that instant, all my nerves were gone. And when he started to lead me to my bedroom, I didn't resist.

———

It was awful. Not Brandon. He was respectful and attentive, but I couldn't get past the fact that I was trying to force myself to do something I didn't want to do. We'd fallen into bed and were deep into the make-out session when he started to peel my clothes off. At that point, I should've just gotten it over with. But instead, I'd freaked out. The moment he'd pulled my shirt open, I'd jumped up and wrapped myself in a robe.

Poor guy. He'd been understanding, and when I'd asked for some time to myself, he'd kissed the top of my head and asked if he should leave. I'd wanted to say yes. Wanted to walk him to the door and send him on his way. But I couldn't. If I rejected Brandon, I'd just have to find someone else.

In the end, I'd gone through with it, but it had been awkward and impersonal. For the first time in my life, I truly resented being a sex witch. If this was what I had to do in order to work with my sister and the coven, it wasn't worth it.

"Everything okay?" Brandon asked as he tied his shoelaces. He was moving slowly, as if he'd just woken up. His lethargic movements made me feel guilty for taking his energy. He'd recover, but it would be a few days.

"Yeah, sure." I pulled a bulky sweater over my head and stuffed my feet into a pair of boots. "I really appreciate—"

He put his hand up, cutting off my words. "Don't."

I raised my eyebrows in question.

He shoved his hands in his jeans pockets. "Look. We both know you didn't want to do this. And if it weren't for the fact that I knew you needed this to get strong, I wouldn't have gone through with it."

"You wouldn't have?" I sat on the edge of my bed and rubbed at the stabbing pain that had formed over my left eye.

He let out an ironic chuckle. "No one wants to be second choice, Mati."

"What? You're not second choice. You were my first choice. This isn't about wanting someone else. It was about who I could trust."

He sat down next to me. "I believe that's what you think. And I know you trust me," he said, his tone gruff with fatigue. He kissed the back of my hand and then tucked it between both of his. "But pretty soon I think you're going to realize the reason you're not that into this is because you're wishing you were with someone else."

I pulled my hand from his. "You don't know what you're talking about."

He watched me for a moment. "That might be true." He leaned in and kissed my cheek once again, then got up. "Take care, Matisse."

I nodded and let him go. After the front door closed behind him, I ran for my shower and spent the next half hour under the scalding-hot water.

By the time I emerged from my bathroom, my skin was bright red and the afternoon seemed like a vague memory. The only evidence that Brandon and I had been together was the magic coursing through my veins.

My magic. It was back. Thank the Goddess. I grabbed my phone.

Chessa answered on the first ring. "Mati?"

"I'm ready. Meet me in ten minutes."

"I'll be there."

———

"Are you sure about this?" Chessa asked as we stared at the portal in the shadow world.

"Yes." The more I thought about it, the more determined I was. Chessa wanted this. If the portals were closed, there wouldn't be a need for demon hunters and Vaughn and his ilk would be out of business.

"Okay. I have another spell to try. It has more juice."

I nodded. "Sounds good. I'm ready when you are." But then nervous energy skittered through me. "What if we summon another demon?"

"I took care of the last one. Don't worry."

"Are you forgetting one came after me?"

"Right. We'll cast a protection spell. Or maybe a deflection spell." She grabbed my hand and squeezed. "I won't let that happen again."

Her matter-of-fact, no-nonsense tone put me at ease. "Then let's get this done."

"I did some research. It appears you need to be the sole spell caster. All I can do is back you up if a demon comes forward. You cool with that?"

"Yep. I got this." I'd almost closed the portal last time. With a little more finesse, I could make it happen. I was sure of it.

"Good. Show me what you've got." Her eyes were bright with excitement. I knew how much this meant to her. She'd lost a good friend to a demon. That was worse than anything I'd gone through.

With determination, I raised my hands over my head and concentrated on the outline of the portal.

"*Obfirmave*," I cried and poured every last bit of my energy into the spell. This time instead of the light flickering, it turned a brilliant bright white. The light called to me, invaded me, and made me one with the spell.

Everything disappeared. All I saw was magic pulsing around me.

Chessa was gone. The shadow world was gone.

All that was left was power.

I flung my head back and let the seductive energy ripple through me. It was heady and made me feel so incredibly *alive*.

I'd never wielded that much power before. Never been so connected with a spell before. I didn't want to let it go. I could have stayed suspended there in that moment forever. I would have too. It was that mesmerizing.

But then I felt a tug, and my magic started to slip away. No! Panic took over. I would *not* lose my power again. No one, not even a demon, was going to pry it from me.

The portal. I had to close it. Now. My power pulsed around me, and then with a burst of energy, I cast everything I had at the portal.

Chessa said something, but I couldn't make out her words. I was too focused. All I saw was light shining back at me.

"Close, dammit," I demanded.

Tears of sheer emotion burned my eyes. I had to do this. My heart ached too much not to. It was my way of making peace with the fact that I was a sex witch. Ever since Vaughn happened, I'd felt dirty. Using people for power was awful. I wouldn't do it again. But if I could close this one portal, make the world safer, maybe I could be right with myself again.

My magic burst forth with one final effort. The brilliant white light vanished. The portal was gone, too. The wall was solid black, with no outline of light. I'd done it. It was closed. I turned to Chessa, bouncing with excitement.

"You did it! Oh my Goddess. I can't believe it." She flung her arms around me as we both squealed.

"Believe it." I laughed out of sheer relief and pulled back. "This changes everything."

She nodded, but as I watched her, Chessa's image started to fade. One moment she was solid, then I could see right through her. "Chessa?"

"Mati?" She looked just as confused as I felt.

"What's going on?" I asked, but it was too late. Chessa had faded away completely.

Suddenly all the magic I'd just used slammed back into me, burning through my veins. I writhed and twisted, screaming in pain, unable to cast it off. It was consuming me, charring me from the inside out. This was it. I was going to die right there in the shadow world. The pain was so intense I almost welcomed the end. But then my fight reflex kicked in. I couldn't give up. Not now.

Without knowing what else to do, I forced the burning sensation from my mind and concentrated on the riverfront. I needed to get home. Needed to get to my coven. I took two steps, willing myself back through the shadows. Then everything fled and the river-scented air hit me. Only I didn't land on the west bank of the Mississippi. I was on the east bank, or what I thought was the east bank, near the French Quarter. The only problem was no one else was there.

The pain was gone. It had vanished the moment I'd left the shadow world. Nothing was left except the horrific memory. I spun, looking for a tourist or cars going across the nearby bridge. There was nothing. The world was deserted. This had to be some sort of alternate reality. My heart sped up. Where was I? I had to get back to my world. Panic took over at the thought of stepping back into the shadows, but I couldn't stay where I was.

I sucked in a breath and told myself the spell was broken. Whatever had happened wouldn't happen again. It couldn't if I didn't cast any more magic.

Tamping down my panic, I let my eyes slide out of focus as I concentrated on the shadows. Only when I took the step to cross over, instead of slipping back into the shadows, a thick fog rushed in and I was trapped in a world of nothing but gray.

I flung my hands out, trying in vain to clear the fog as I stumbled backward and forward, searching for a break in visibility. No luck.

Shit! Now what?

Magic. As much as I didn't want to call on that particular gift at the moment, it was my last and only resource. Gritting my teeth, I raised my arms over my head, pictured my apartment, and yelled, "Return!"

Nothing. Not even a tingle. My heart started to pound against my chest. No magic? Terrified, I reached deep in my gut for my power. I couldn't feel even the tiniest spark. A cold, terrifying realization came over me. My magic was gone and I was trapped in some void world. There was no way out.

My only hope was that Chessa would find a way to bring me home.

Chapter 16

Vaughn

I was working at the motorcycle shop when Mitch's name popped up on my cell phone. Now what? I'd already suffered through two rants about how I'd fucked up the last mission. Never mind that Waters was safely locked away and wasn't getting out anytime soon. Apparently the information about the Black Heart curse was more important than keeping women safe from jackasses who thought nothing of using their fists to win an argument.

"Vaughn," he said after I answered. "I have a time-sensitive job for you. Can you handle it?" His tone was a little testy, but nothing worse than normal.

"Depends on what it is."

"There's a witch who's casting black magic. He just left here. I need you to pick him up."

I grabbed a pen. "Name?"

"Lucien Boulard."

I frowned. "Weren't you friends with a guy by that name?"

"Sort of. Same guy. And he just tried to curse me. Pick him up and bring him to me."

I swallowed my snarky reply. "I will if no Council witches show up out of the blue."

"Make sure of it. I want to question him first. Consider it a courtesy since we knew each other once. Be careful, though. He's a lot more powerful than most." Mitch paused, and when he spoke again, I could hear the sneer in his tone. "Just don't fuck it up this time."

I ignored the barb. He could be pissed all he wanted. It wasn't going to change things. "Last known location?"

"The abandoned Six Flags."

"Six Flags? What were you doing there?"

He cleared his throat. "I've been dabbling in the movie-making business. Just a side job. Never mind that. Bring me Boulard and you're in for a bonus."

The line went dead. Bonus? Right. I'd be lucky to get one red cent out of him. He still hadn't paid me for the last job. Maybe Mitch would get over himself if I brought him Boulard. But if he was as powerful as Mitch seemed to think, I couldn't take any chances. I'd have to neutralize him before he even knew I was there. Otherwise, if he wanted to, he could kill me.

I sat at my computer and ran the trace on his car registration. Five minutes later a map with a flashing icon popped up on the screen. Boulard was on the move. I took careful notes of which route he was traveling. Even though I didn't know where he was going, if I tracked him for any amount of time, patterns would form.

So far he was just tooling around town. Nothing special. Except when he finally stopped. "No way," I mumbled. The bastard was parked right in front of the motorcycle shop. Interesting. Did he know he was being tracked?

It didn't matter. He was on my turf. After grabbing my phone and keys, I took off in the SUV. Ten minutes later, I parked a block and a half down from where Boulard's car was sitting. What was he doing? Using my binoculars, I focused in on him. Nothing. He was just waiting. Waiting for me no doubt. What else would he be doing there? Did he think he was going to use me against Mitch? Not if I had anything to say about it.

I hit a button on my phone and called the shop. "Hey, boss?"

"Paxton. Why are you bothering me?"

I grinned. "Because if I don't, no one else will."

"Tell the old lady that."

"Not on your life. Listen. I need a favor."

The boss mumbled something about pain-in-the-ass employees, then said, "Well? I don't have all day."

Suppressing a chuckle, I cleared my throat. "Right. You see that guy sitting outside your shop in a Jeep?"

"The pretty boy who looks like he needs to get laid?"

There was no stopping the laugh this time. "Yep. That one."

"He's waiting for you."

Well, that was interesting. "Good. Can you go out there and wave him in. Don't approach him, just yell that I came in through the back or something."

"Did you?"

"What? Come in the back?"

"Yeah. Are you here?" he asked.

"I'm outside," I said.

"Right. And you can't approach him because?"

"He's a douche who's casing the place." I stole another glance at him through the binoculars. "I'm going to take him out before he gets a chance."

"I knew there was a reason I hired your ugly ass. You want me to do it now?"

"Give me five minutes."

The line went dead. I grabbed my zip ties, a Taser, and a dart. If I did this right, he'd never know what hit him. Mitch had mentioned he was powerful and a black-magic user. I couldn't take a chance. If at all possible, I'd use the dart. It was only a small pinch that would put him out for less than ten minutes. If things got ugly, I'd go for the Taser.

Keeping a close eye on the Jeep, I exited my SUV and then jogged around the block so I was coming at the Jeep from behind. The boss still hadn't poked his head out yet, so I cut between two of the houses, acting as if I belonged there.

Before long, I heard Rick shout to Boulard. Time to move. With the dart clutched in one hand and the Taser in my pocket, I strode out from between the houses and came up behind my target just as he was exiting his car. "Mr. Boulard?" I asked, making sure I had the right guy.

He turned. "Yes?"

"Thanks for stopping by." I held my hand out as if I was going to shake his hand, but before he could react, I jabbed the dart into his forearm.

His eyes widened and then went dark with anger. Magic crackled at his palms but just as quickly vanished. A second later, his eyes rolled into the back of his head as he collapsed at my feet.

I waved at my boss. "I'll get him to the authorities."

"Good deal. See you tomorrow."

I reached down, hauled Boulard up, and then stuffed him back in his car. He could wait there while I got my SUV.

Matisse

Time seemed to stand still in my world of fog. There was no way to know if days or nights had passed. It was an endless stream of gray and nothingness. I felt nothing. Not even the pangs of hunger. Just despair at being trapped in a world of silence.

I was lying on the hard ground when I sensed a disturbance followed by a thud. I sat straight up, my heart racing. Had Chessa found me? Or had a demon found a way in? My breath came in short bursts as I waited, frozen in fear and hope.

"Kane?" a female voice called.

Kane? Who was that?

"Kane?" The woman's voice was frantic now. There was some swearing and then I felt a brush of magic. It was warm and inviting, pushing my fear away.

I moved in the direction of the voice, desperate to find this woman, whoever she was. Anything was better than being in this place alone. Since I could feel her magic I said, "Banish the mist."

"What? Who are you?" she asked.

Slightly irritated, I called back, "Who are you?"

"Mati? Is that you?"

Oh, Goddess. She knew who I was. I opened my mouth to speak, but no words formed. I was too overwhelmed. Someone had come for me.

"Matisse? If that's you, your sister sent me. Chessandra."

Tears welled in my eyes. Chessa hadn't abandoned me.

The other woman ranted something about it being her wedding day while I tried to compose myself.

When she started to wonder aloud about my identity, I forced myself to speak. "It's your wedding day?" Compassion filled me for this woman. And I thought my life had been disrupted.

"Well, not anymore."

"Damn. That sucks. Chessa's such a bitch." The words were some sort of defense mechanism to keep myself from falling apart. Chessa had pulled out all the stops to make sure I made it home.

"Yes, it does. And yes, she is."

I felt bad for her, but if she could get me out of here, I'd personally reschedule everything for her wedding. "Are you a witch? Or just a shadow walker?" I asked. Her cluelessness earlier made me wonder. The magic I felt could be from either. Shadow walkers had just enough magic to bounce between worlds.

"Both. Now what did you mean when you said to banish the mist?"

"You need to cast a banishing spell." How was it possible she didn't know what that was? It was a basic skill. "You said you're a witch, right?"

She let out a huff. "Yes. But I don't normally banish things unless we're talking about evil spirits."

That amused me and a small laugh bubbled out. She could banish ghosts, but not mist. I knew who this was. That white witch, Jade Calhoun, who'd come to town not too long ago and hadn't even known she was a witch. She'd taken over as coven leader for the New Orleans coven when Bea stepped down. No wonder she was the one who was here. Not many were as powerful as she was.

I guess my laughter irritated her because she said, "Look. If you want my help, you might want to start cooperating. Otherwise, I'm out of here."

Crap. That was pretty grumpy. I guess I would've been too if my wedding had been interrupted. "You're the white witch, aren't you?"

"Yes." There was a bit of hesitation in her tone.

"Figures." I let out a sigh and sat, too exhausted to keep standing. It wasn't comforting that I knew more than she did. "This is the spell. *By my mind, by my heart, by the power of my will, may the mists part.*"

"Okay… but why don't you do it?"

"I can't." Anger welled in my chest. "My magic has… well, it's not working."

"Oh." Then she repeated the words and the mist parted.

I turned, catching sight of the pretty strawberry-blond witch. She radiated with power as she frantically searched the area.

"No! Dammit, this was not supposed to happen," she said.

I turned to her. "What wasn't supposed to happen?"

"Kane is supposed to be here. He jumped through with me. Where is he?"

Standing, I moved closer to her. "Unless this Kane is a powerful witch, he likely can't come here."

"Where are we?"

I shrugged. "Damned if I know. But it doesn't mist in the shadow world, and this place is void of other souls."

Fear rippled over her face. "We're not in Purgatory, are we?"

I'd wondered that myself, but had ruled that out. "No. This… feels different."

She cast about for a couple of other explanations and I answered as best I could, but really all I could think about was getting home. The rest of it was details I didn't care about.

Finally she said, "I'm going to get you out of here."

I raised my eyebrows. "How?"

"However I leave, you're coming with me." She furrowed her brow. "How did you end up here? That portal was a gate to Hell."

I sat back down and buried my head in my hands. Seriously? Couldn't she just cast a spell? I jerked my head up. "I was working on closing the veil from the shadow world to Hell. Chessandra's orders." This was the last thing I wanted to talk about right now. But if she was going to get us out of here, the information might help. "The spell seemed to work, too, but then it backfired and rushed through me." I shuddered. "I was on fire. It literally felt like I was burning alive. I thought I was going to die."

Tears were flowing freely now due to my ordeal. When it had just been me, all by myself, I'd been able to block everything out, but now that I was talking about it, I couldn't hold back the horror.

The witch was kind as she gently asked more questions and promised help from her coven.

I stiffened. "I don't think that's going to work."

"Sure it will. We just need to get you out of here."

I'd do just about anything to leave, but she had to know the facts before she made promises she couldn't keep. Her coven would never help the likes of me. Not a sex witch. "I belong to the witches of Coven Pointe."

"So?" She shrugged as if it didn't matter.

I fidgeted. "You don't know, do you?"

Sighing, she ran a hand through her long hair and then rolled her eyes. "Obviously not. Why don't you fill me in on whatever it is?"

She was so clueless and yet seemed so sincere. I couldn't help but like her. "You're the white witch who took over for

Beatrice and you have no idea. This is just…" I shook my head. "She sure has her secrets. The witches of Coven Pointe live across the river."

"You mean Algiers Point?"

I raised an eyebrow. "We call it Coven Pointe. Have you ever been there?"

"No."

I figured as much. Most of the east bank witches didn't have any reason to visit us. "There's a reason for that. Before Algiers Point was founded, it was claimed by my ancestors and was called Coven Pointe. Over time, they were driven out. But fifty years ago, my grandmother and her siblings reclaimed what is ours. We've been at war—if you will—with the New Orleans coven ever since."

"What?" A look of skepticism crossed her features. "Do your people dabble in black magic?"

"No," I said, pissed she'd even asked.

"Thank the Goddess for that."

I went on to explain we were more experimental than most. It had to do with our sex magic. But that wasn't the real reason we had conflict. It was an old grudge between my aunt and Beatrice. No one really knew why.

"That seems… crazy. No offense," she said.

I agreed, but what was I going to do about it?

"Never mind," she said. "Let's just get out of here and we'll figure it out later."

A moment later, I was clutching the white witch's hand as magic swirled around her. This was it. I would be home in a matter of moments. Her magic brightened, almost blinding me. I clung to her hand, determined to cross over with her.

But as she took a step forward, it was as if there was an invisible wall. All I could do was watch as she slipped through it. The fog rushed in around me, trapping me once more in my gray prison.

Chapter 17

Vaughn

Boulard was unconscious for the entire ride over to Mitch's house. At least I didn't have to worry about him spelling me.

I waited outside Mitch's house until the witch's eyes fluttered open. He blinked and then shook his head as if to clear the cobwebs.

"Who are you?" he asked, his eyes bloodshot.

"Just a guy hired to do a job." I got out of the SUV. Even though it was weird to bring a target directly to Mitch's house, I dismissed the thought. If he wanted to question Boulard first, he was free to do so. I dragged the witch out of the passenger's seat.

"Who hired you?" he demanded, straightening as the last of the drug wore off.

I said nothing and pushed him up the steps. I had no sympathy for black-magic users.

"You're making a mistake. I'm a member of the New Orleans coven. When they find out about this—"

I kicked the door open and hauled him inside, expecting to find Mitch back at his computer as always. But instead what I found was a horror film in progress. Or what should have been a horror film.

Mitch was standing over a woman whose hands were bound. While she wasn't actively building power, white light pulsed around her, indicating a powerful white witch. In contrast, black magic clung to Mitch. Holy fuck. What was he doing?

Another woman was sprawled on the floor, clearly in pain.

"Mitch? What's going on?"

"None of your damned business. Leave Boulard and go."

I'd never seen Mitch use dark magic before. And by the way he was glaring at me, I was certain he was too far gone to reason with. I glanced around, realizing if I didn't do something, these people would likely die. I tamped down the rage consuming me and forced myself to keep my cool. Instinct told me if I challenged Mitch now, I'd be his next casualty with no way to help these people.

"Where do you want him?" I asked Mitch, glancing from the woman on the floor to the one at Mitch's feet. I recognized her. Jade Calhoun. I'd made it my business to know who the most powerful witches in the city were. I couldn't stop my next words. "What the hell, Mitch? Why do you have a white witch bound like that?"

"You can tell what I am?" she asked, her eyes wide and pleading.

"It's a gift of mine," I lied, kneeling in front of her. "Why are you here?"

Mitch scoffed. "She's here because she broke into my house."

She scowled up at him, pain contorting her face. How had he managed to neutralize her? And why was he wielding black magic as if it was second nature? Son of a bitch. This couldn't be the first time he'd used black magic. He must have gone over the edge a long time ago.

Keeping my expression neutral, I stood. "What did she want?"

"She was looking for him." Mitch pointed to Lucien. "I guess she thought he was already here."

She lifted her head, shooting eye daggers at Mitch. "I came for—"

Mitch waved his hand, flinging a giant ball of magic. The witch gasped and curled into herself. He'd just gut-punched her with magic. Animal. I wanted to tear him apart. Would've too, if the three other people weren't present. It was too dangerous for them. I knew I couldn't beat him. But one solid punch would feel damn good.

Fuck. I'd never in my life wished I had supernatural abilities as much as I did right then. A voice whispered in my head. *If you'd accepted your spot with the Brotherhood...*

"She's being difficult." Mitch eyed me. "How did she know you were bringing the witch? Did you tell anyone you were working for me?"

I cast Mitch a bored expression, keeping up my act. "I don't tell anyone about my work." Glancing at the witch, I tried to keep the scowl off my face. Did he have any idea who she was? "You know she's the coven leader, right?"

"No, she isn't. The old lady took over again. But I've got this covered. You can go now."

Every instinct told me Mitch had gone over the edge. He was dealing in some dark shit, and these hostages were paying the price. I continued to do everything I could to appear uncaring even though rage was burning through my veins. I had to if there was any chance of getting out of there and finding help. I held out my hand. "Payment."

Mitch scowled. "Fuckin' A. You know I'm good for it."

"Payment on delivery. Those were the terms. If you ever expect to use my services again, you'll make good on the deal." I didn't want to test him, but on any other day I would. If I let it go now, he might get suspicious.

Mitch reluctantly pulled out a wad of money from his front pocket and handed a stack of hundreds to me. Now I knew he was fucking around with dark forces. It's the only way he'd have that kind of cash. I pocketed the money and turned to leave, anxious to make a phone call or two.

"Hey!" the witch at Mitch's feet called. "None of this is what you think. Mitch kidna—oomph." Mitch planted his foot in her ribs, and I had to use every last bit of will to not rip his head off. I wanted to. I didn't give a shit what happened to me. But Mitch's hostages? He was already all too willing to torture them.

"Shut up," he said. "Lying bitch. She can't seem to separate fact from fiction." Mitch's voice was cool, dispassionate, as if today was just another day. "I've got it from here."

I took one last look at the two women and then glanced at Boulard. If Mitch did anything to permanently hurt any of them while I was gone, I'd never forgive myself.

The door slammed behind me, and I broke out into a dead run. Once I was back at my SUV, I placed a call to Maximus. I hadn't seen any demons, but Mitch's eyes had flashed red. That was a sure sign he was dealing with them. I couldn't take any chances.

"Vaughn." Maximus answered on the first ring.

"You need to send a crew to Mitch's house. He's dealing in black magic. He's got three people held captive."

There was a pause on the other end. "That's really a job for the Witches' Council."

I stifled the urge to growl at him. "I don't think you under-stand. His eyes are flashing red and he has a white witch tied up. I could call the Council, but they have a history of running things by committee. This can't wait for them to decide who to send. These people need action now."

"A white witch?" His tone was deadly serious. "Jade Calhoun?"

"Yeah. Her and two of her friends."

"I'll have a crew there in ten minutes."

Relief flooded me. "Faster, if possible."

"Stay there. Keep an eye on the house. If anyone leaves the structure, call me back."

"Got it."

I tucked the phone in my pocket and sat there in my SUV, completely rigid as I watched the clock tick. By the time five minutes had gone by, I was ready to crawl out of my skin. Waiting and doing nothing was killing me.

When the clock hit eight minutes, four men wielding long daggers materialized out of thin air right in front of Mitch's house. Without pausing, they burst inside. The battle seemed to last forever, but after ten minutes the house was quiet.

My phone rang. Maximus. "Hello," I said.

"You were right. There were two demons. The crew has them under control."

"Okay. Good." I gripped the steering wheel. "And Mitch?"

"He got away. Ran out the back door. You should probably go before he sees you watching his house."

"I can't leave without apprehending him. What he did…" The images turned my stomach. "He's out of control."

"No doubt. But maybe you shouldn't be the one to bring him in."

I appreciated what he was saying. But why not me? To spare my parents? They'd be horrified if they knew what he was up to. And nothing would give me more satisfaction than bringing him down. After what he'd done today? Yeah. Nothing. Still, I told the old man what he wanted to hear. Mitch was gone anyway. I was confident I could find him. My best course of action was to lay low, put a trace on him, and be patient. If the demon hunters had gotten the demons, Mitch would be out of commission for a while. "Okay. Thanks for the help."

"Thank you," he said. "You know, you'd make one hell of a demon hunter."

I wasn't ready to admit it, but the idea no longer seemed as awful as it once had. If I'd been a hunter, I could've helped sooner. "I'll be in touch."

"I hope so."

━━━

A few hours later, I got a message that the white witch wanted to meet with me. It was the least I could do after what I'd allowed to happen at my brother's house. Aware that she was a high-profile witch and wanting to keep my new house as undercover as possible, I sent her to another address first as part of a diversionary tactic in case she was being followed.

An hour later, I was fresh from the shower when a knock sounded at my door. I pulled on clean jeans and headed to greet my guests.

The strawberry-blond witch stood with Boulard, a woman with curly red hair, and Beatrice Kelton, the longtime New Orleans coven leader. "Mr. Paxton?" Jade said. "I believe you were expecting us."

I flashed her a smile. "Ms. Calhoun. It's good to see you well. Our last meeting… uh, that was an unpleasant piece of business. I'm glad the Brotherhood was able to get the situation under control."

Lucien scowled. "Under control? You're the one who delivered me there."

My smile vanished. He had every right to hate my guts. "My apologies to you, Mr. Boulard. I can assure you that as soon as I assessed the situation, I called in the Brotherhood." I opened the door wider. "Please, come in where we can talk."

Jade glanced around outside. "No offense, but you do realize we could be being watched, right? I mean anyone staking out your apartment could've just followed us. Your wild goose chase seems a little pointless."

I laughed, loving her spunk. "They could've, but why would they? As far as they know, you came by my apartment, realized I wasn't home, and left. Besides, there's a spell on this house. Only those invited can see it. We're all safe here. Don't worry about it. Have a seat."

I led them though my sparsely furnished house until we got to my couch and two club chairs.

Jade introduced me to her friend Kat, and Beatrice and I exchanged hellos. Then they turned their attention to Jade. She was clearly in charge.

"I'm here for two reasons," she said. "They are both of equal importance, but one matter is more pressing." She waved to Lucien. "He's been spelled with a Black Heart curse. One person has already died. And now one of these two"—she indicated Lucien and Kat with a wave to each of them—"is next."

"A Black Heart curse?" Narrowing my eyes, I studied Lucien. And deep in my gut, I knew Mitch was a part of whatever had happened to him. Mitch's anger at not being able to question Sam's attacker was making a lot more sense now. "I see."

"We know who cursed him," Jade said. "We need him in order to reverse it."

I turned to meet her gaze. "And how can I help?"

"It's your brother Mitch. We need you to help us find him."

Nausea rolled through me. My brother *was* responsible for the awful curse. I'd thought he was involved, but hearing it from her lips made me want to vomit. I stood and paced the room. "You're sure it was him?"

"I'm positive," Lucien said. "We were acquaintances back then. He was there when it happened and today he admitted it to me."

"Dammit." I ran my hand through my hair, frustrated. This was going to kill my parents. "This is going to get messy."

"I suspect it is." Jade's tone was low and full of compassion. But her next words were straight and to the point. "And since the Brotherhood didn't take him down, I imagine he's on the run or in a safe house until this blows over."

I sat back down. "I can probably take you to him." I'd already started my trace and had some leads.

Beatrice gave me a grim smile. "You're sure about that? You'll be signing your brother's death warrant before long."

I met her eyes with a cold, hard stare. "Ms. Kelton, I'm an undercover agent. It's my job to take down those who make deals with the devil."

She regarded me for a minute and then nodded. "Understood."

Turning my attention to Jade, I asked, "What's the second piece of business?"

"It's Matisse."

Mati? Was she hurt? Fear sliced through my chest as I sat up straighter. Had a demon come for her again?

"She's trapped in a void world and we need you to help her cross back over." Jade kept her penetrating stare on me.

She was in trouble. And her magic wasn't one hundred percent. Shit! That was my fault. Self-loathing gripped me and wouldn't let go. "Trapped?"

"Yes, and she'll fade away into nothing if we don't get her out soon."

"And why do you need me?" I shouldn't be anywhere near her. I'd broken the strong, sexy witch with my incubus curse. Damn the Brotherhood. Damn my destiny.

"Dayla says you stole something from her. And in order for her to cross, she needs it back."

"What?" I stood. "Stole? I took nothing from her." But even as I said the words, I knew that was wrong. I'd taken her magic. But I didn't have it now. How could I give it back?

She gave me a sympathetic smile. "But you did. Do you know what kind of witch she is?"

"Yes." She knew. They all knew. Son of a…

She leaned in and lowered her voice. "Did you know that after the last time you saw her, she spent a month recuperating?"

Hearing the words, the nonjudgmental way she said them, only served to heighten my self-hatred. Yeah, I knew. And now this woman was confirming whatever happened to her was my fault. Fuck.

There were a million questions on the tip of my tongue. I wanted to know how Matisse had ended up in another world. And why. But none of that mattered. We had to get to her. "I'll do whatever's necessary. Now if you'll excuse me, I need to get dressed." I strode off to the back of the house, calling over my shoulder, "We'll leave in five minutes. Be prepared."

Chapter 18

Vaughn

In the end, it didn't take very long to track Mitch down. The magic he'd been wielding must've fried his brain because he'd chosen to hide out in an empty rental that was owned by our parents.

I knew he was there as soon as we pulled up. It was the way the curtains were closed in the front. When it was empty, my parents were careful to keep them open for drive-by renters. I convinced the group to let me go in first. Told them I'd distract him to make the raid go easier.

My rage for what had gone down today consumed me, and as stupid as it was, I wanted to take a shot at him before the magical showdown. He wouldn't run out on me. Why would he? He knew he could overpower me with that magic of his. I didn't give a shit. As long as he didn't kill me before I could help Matisse, he could do his worst. I knew I would.

Not caring if he heard me, I strolled right through the front door. "Mitch," I called. Better he knew it was me. Maybe then he wouldn't come out magic blazing like he would if he thought the Brotherhood was still after him.

"What the fuck are you doing here?" he said from the threshold to the long hallway.

"Looking for you."

"Why? Planning on leading more meddlesome do-gooders my way?" The red was gone from his eyes, but his sneer was proof enough of his loyalties.

"Are you planning on torturing anymore innocent witches?" I wasn't holding anything back now. He was going to hear every word I had to say. "Cursing your friends? Really, Mitch? What a bitch move."

"You!" His eyes narrowed as he advanced on me. "You sent those assholes. You ruined everything. And after I kept you afloat all these months with bounty jobs. You ungrateful piece of shit."

I held my ground, waiting until he was less than a foot from me.

"Think I won't spell you, too? Think I'll spare you for good old Mom and Dad? Think again, little brother. I hold all the power here, and you've crossed a line you can't recover from."

"Why did you do it, Mitch? Black magic? You had a sweet deal with the Council. Why ruin it?"

His face contorted with disgust. "Fuck the Council. They treat me just like Rissa did. Zero respect. Boulard and his bitches deserved what they got. Boulard especially. He stole the one person I ever loved." His eyes flashed with buried emotion. "All I wanted to know was why the Black Heart curse that I hit him with failed. Why the white witch was able to neutralize it. Why do you think I wanted to question Sam's attacker? I need to know more about that curse. But you fucked everything up!"

Rissa had been his girlfriend a long time ago. After she left him, I'd heard she died from a freak spell that had backfired, but now it was all coming together. Mitch was responsible. He'd killed her. And all because he'd been dumped. Sick bastard.

I cast him a horrified look. How could I be even remotely related to this monster? Without a word, I swung. My fist hit his jaw with a satisfying crunch. He went down in a heap. The loser. Without his magic he was nothing.

I stood over him, rage still streaming through my veins. "Get up."

He rolled, curling into a ball.

"Jesus." Disgusted, I pulled out my zip ties, ready to apprehend him. Only just as I reached for him, he twisted, and a bolt of magic caught me right in the chest.

Shit!

I collapsed, my entire body numb.

Mitch got to his feet and snarled. "You stupid, idiotic, no-good mama's boy. Don't ever touch me again." Blood dripped from his lip. "By the time I'm done with you, you'll wish I'd given you to the demons."

With me unable to fight back, Mitch dragged me from the living room into a room toward the back of the house. Grunting, he kicked me and spat his blood in my face. I couldn't even flinch and had to endure the sickening ooze as it slid down my temple. Death would've been kinder.

Mitch was eyeing me, and I felt magic growing around him. But before he could attack me again, I heard the boom of the front door crashing open. The witches were here.

With his magic already pooling at his fingertips, Mitch spun and tore through the house. Shouts mingled with heavy footsteps and the sound of magic bouncing off the walls. I lay motionless, utterly frustrated and seething until finally the feeling started to come back into my limbs. I sat up but realized Mitch had cuffed me to an armoire. Goddamn him. I struggled to reach the knife stashed in my boot, but my hands were tied too tight. There was nothing to do but wait.

After what seemed like forever, the white witch finally came for me. She looked no worse for the wear as she asked, "What happened?"

"The bastard spelled me. My fucking brother's a lunatic. He blames me for what happened earlier today. He's figured out it was me that sent the demon hunters. Did you dust his ass?" I asked hopefully.

"First of all, he isn't a vampire. And second, no. We need him in order to force Lucien's curse to reverse itself."

Beatrice came up behind her and with one zap of magic my hands were free of the zip ties.

I rubbed my wrists. "Thanks for saving my ass." Then I staggered to my feet and strode back into the front part of the house, eyeing my piece-of-shit stepbrother. I sat there, doing nothing to help him while the witches forced him to reverse the Black Heart curse on Boulard. The way they worked together and the obvious love they had for each other was like nothing I'd ever experienced before. These witches would die for each other. Had I ever felt that way about anyone? Matisse's image floated into my consciousness. Right then and there I knew I wanted to be that person for her.

When it was all over, they called the Witches' Council and I felt nothing. No grief. No relief. Just resignation. I'd lost a brother today, and I didn't even care.

"See you in the morning?" Jade asked.

I nodded as I headed out. We were going to bring Matisse back. Even if I had to die trying.

—

Matisse

The white witch, Jade, had come to check on me once more. And that's when she dropped the bomb that she was bringing Vaughn to help get me home. I'd instantly resisted, but secretly I wanted to see him. Wanted to rage against him. Make him suffer for what he'd done to me. But at the same time, I just wanted to be near him. Being alone in this world was slowly killing me, and he was the one person I'd connected with. After all I'd been through, I no longer cared about my pride. I only wanted to feel something. Anything. And he was one who could make it happen.

After spending over a week in the void world, I'd started to waste away. The witch had brought me some nourishment pills. They'd given me a small amount of energy, but what had been the real help was the pendant she'd left me. She'd said it might help ground me to her and our world. I think she was right. It was infused with her magic. A magic I could cling to.

I lay on the bank of the river, clutching the pendant to my chest, just letting the power pulse through my hand. Time was nonexistent. All I had to focus on was the magic. It was like a spark waiting to go off. And then it happened. The air rippled around me, and power rushed into me, making me strong. I felt myself stand as wind whipped through my hair. Only the power wasn't normal. It was like a psychedelic high, causing images of a life I hadn't led to flash through my mind.

Me as a little girl sitting on a man's knee. My father. The one I'd never known. Friends surrounding me at a birthday party I'd never had. And Vaughn, saying good-bye to me on the bank of the Mississippi.

"We're not meant for each other, Mati," he said, cold and uncaring.

"You don't mean that," I said softly, refraining from clutching at his shirt.

"I do. I got what I came for. Now you need to lead your life, and I'll lead mine." No emotion rolled behind his eyes. He was a completely different person than the one I'd given myself to.

The pain clutched at my gut and left me hollow. Used. Unloved. "You never cared for me."

He said nothing as he stared at me, his blank expression morphing into one of pity. "Don't, Matisse. You're better than that."

I hated him. Hated everything about him in that moment. He'd used me. Taken my trust. My power. And had left me for dead. The calculating bastard had gotten what he wanted. And I'd meant nothing. Gut-wrenching pain coursed through me. I wanted to scream. To beg him to stay. And I hated myself for it. He'd taken something precious from me. That piece of me that I held close and never gave up. The one I'd given to him freely and he'd stomped on it, leaving me broken and damaged.

I was lost in my pain, uncontrollable foreign magic sparking through me, when I heard a faint feminine voice. "Matisse?"

A war battled inside me as the voice worked to pull me from my vision. I fought it, not wanting to go back to nothing, to my world cloaked in gray. Power rushed through my limbs, and a bolt of lightning struck somewhere near me, crackling over the river.

"Matisse," the voice insisted, compelling me to jerk my head in her direction. I stared at the wide-eyed witch, waiting to see what she wanted.

"You're okay," she said, taking tentative steps toward me. "We've come to take you home."

"I don't have a home," I said, shifting my gaze past her to the one person I both hated and wanted to run to. "He stole it."

"Who? Vaughn?"

I laughed humorlessly, still feeling the remnants of the vision. "You could say that."

"Mati," Vaughn said, his voice enticing and seductive in the worst possible way. His body was calling to me, making me want him. I couldn't let that happen.

I stiffened, letting the power build around me. The glow shifted from pale blue to a brilliant purple as I focused on him. "You're not welcome here." I meant the words to be a command, but they came out soft and tentative.

He took two steps and was in front of me, clasping his hands lightly around my wrists. My arms cooled with his touch, bringing me back to myself. Love and desperation warred for dominance in my heart. "Why did you come?" I demanded, angry at the way he could make me feel things I never wanted to feel again.

"To restore what I took from you."

The reminder of his betrayal sent me into a frenzy, unraveling any last shred of self-control that I had. The magic burst from my fingertips, owning me, using me, until all I felt was the sweet release of power.

Crack! The rocks beneath my feet rumbled as the magic tore through them. And through it all, I kept my gaze locked on Vaughn's.

He raised his hand, holding it out to me, and said in the most soothing voice possible, "Come back from that place, Mati. Don't let it take you."

As I stared at him, something shifted inside me. The visions slowly faded away, taking the pain and utter heartache with them. The world started to right itself, and Vaughn, the decent guy I'd given myself to, stood before me, offering himself. He'd give me anything he had in order to save me. I knew it deep in my heart. Could feel it deep in my bones.

I slowly leaned into him, and when his arms finally came around me, tears burned my eyes. He cradled me, whispering, "Everything's going to be all right now. I'm here to bring you home."

He'd come for me. The scene at the river wasn't real. I hadn't been abandoned. Vaughn's arms tightened around me. I pulled back to gaze at him, to see his intention in his eyes. And there I found love. Passion. Protectiveness.

Vaughn's gaze turned soft as he searched my face. His look was so tender, so focused, that I brought my hand up and lightly caressed his cheek. The stubble beneath my fingers was so real it grounded me, solidified that he'd come for me.

"I'm here to give you what I took from you," he said again, his tone so low I barely heard him. "And I won't leave here without you. Not ever. You belong in our world... with me." As he said the last words, he stroked my neck and the spot where he'd marked me. Instantly my insides lit with a small bolt of desire. He *had* marked me. The bruise was gone, but the memory never would be.

"I didn't know," Vaughn said. "I wouldn't have—"

I placed my finger over his lips, silencing him.

He kissed my palm softly, then pulled me to him abruptly, holding me close.

I barely noticed as the white witch and her companion stepped out of this world, leaving me and Vaughn alone. All I could focus on was the man who'd come for me when no one else could. "I thought you didn't want anything to do with me," I said, unable to go on before I knew the truth. "You took my magic and left."

Pain filled his dark eyes. "Not on purpose. I wouldn't have ever left if I'd had a choice. The Brotherhood spelled me and took me from you. I had no idea that was going to happen. I didn't know what I was. What I am. All I knew was that I wanted to be with you." He scanned my face, peering at me, searching for something.

I couldn't give it to him. Not yet.

He closed his eyes and took a deep breath. When he opened them, he continued. "By the time I was able to get away, you were already recovering with your family. I wanted to see you but thought I should wait until you were stronger. But then you were gone again. I fucked up. I should've come as soon as I was able. I apologize. It won't happen again."

It was what Chessa had tried to tell me. And the fact that he was here now was all the proof I needed. He was an incubus. A man who, through no fault of his own, had taken my power and was here to give it back.

I could live with that.

"Kiss me," I said.

And then he did. His lips were soft, testing at first as he kissed the corner of my mouth. But I turned into him, pressing my lips to his. And as his tongue slipped over mine, magic sparked from him to me. My magic. The power I'd been harnessing before had belonged to the white witch. It had given me strength but at a price. A distorted reality. But now that I had a thread of my own, hers had vanished.

I was me again. If not whole, then not broken either. With each caress, each kiss, my power grew. And as our desire heightened, so did my strength.

The world around us vanished. I no longer saw the empty waterfront. Everything narrowed to just me and Vaughn and the heat between us. I wanted him. Needed what he had to give. "Make love to me," I said.

He pulled back and for the briefest moment, I saw a flicker of fear in his gaze.

"You won't hurt me." I knew it deep in my gut. He was here to give, not take. I could feel it. "It's the only way you're going to be able to give me back enough power to let me cross." My magic had been building, but I was still weak. And as a sex witch, I knew what I needed to get strong. He knew it too. I saw it in his eyes.

After a few moments, he pulled me to him, resting his chin on the top of my head. "I'll do anything you need."

"I know," I said, believing he would.

Epilogue

Matisse

In the end, Vaughn did make love to me on the shores of the Mississippi. He was gentle and attentive, giving me everything he had, never once taking pleasure for himself. Not even when I tried to give it to him. He insisted he was making love to me. Not the other way around. And while I felt odd about it, I knew he was making sure he took nothing from me, ensuring that I got my power back. And boy did I.

By the time he finished, I was utterly satisfied in every way and brimming with more power than I'd known what to do with. Vaughn, on the other hand, looked a little pale. Still, with his new incubus powers, he had no trouble jumping with me back into our world.

That was two weeks ago. I'd seen Vaughn numerous times, but only briefly when he stopped by to make sure I was still okay. I was. More than okay, actually. Tonight was the first night we'd actually made plans.

He showed up at my door at eight o'clock sharp with a pitiful-looking bouquet of what appeared to have been sunflowers in another life.

I laughed as I waved him in and eyed his Indian. "Umm, rough ride?"

"You could say that." He dipped his head and kissed me softly.

Heat seared through me as it always did when I was near him. I tamped it down though. We were taking things slow. "Maybe flowers and motorcycles don't mix."

He gave me a wounded look. "I still get points for trying, though, right?"

"Absolutely." I took the mangled stalks and deposited them in my kitchen. When I returned, I slipped an arm around his waist and tilted my head up. "So, what did you want to tell me?" When he'd called to ask if I was busy, he'd said he had news.

He tugged me to sit down next to him on the couch and as he stroked my arm he asked, "How would you feel about having a boyfriend who works for the Brotherhood?"

My brain couldn't get past the word boyfriend. Was he serious?

"Mati?" he asked after I bit my lip.

"Yeah? Oh. The Brotherhood. You mean you want to be a demon hunter?"

He sat back. "Not want. Am. I made it official today."

I tilted my head up, studying him. Shit. I'd read that all wrong. He wasn't asking me if I was okay with him being a demon hunter. He was asking me to be his girlfriend.

He grinned, waiting for my answer.

Goddess. Girlfriend? Did I want that? Was I ready for that? I knew right away the answer was yes. "You know there's going to be a constant power struggle, right?"

His eyes sparked with molten desire as he lowered his lips to mine and whispered, "I wouldn't have it any other way."

I shook my head, chuckling. "You have no idea what you're in for."

"Neither do you."

And then he kissed me, giving me just a taste of what was to come.

About the Author

USA Today bestselling author, Deanna Chase, is a native Californian, transplanted to the slower paced lifestyle of southeastern Louisiana. When she isn't writing, she is often goofing off with her husband in New Orleans, playing with her two shih tzu dogs, making glass beads, or out hocking her wares at various bead shows across the country. For more information and updates on newest releases visit her website at www.deannachase.com